DUST ON THEIR WINGS

A Novel

JEFF MINICK

ISBN: 1517523559
ISBN 13: 9781517523558

To you who have lived and loved with passion,
The living and the dead,
The wise and the foolish,
The starry-eyed, the soul-broken,
The kith and kin whose errant hearts
Never abandoned the quest—

To you I dedicate this book.

What are angels?
Angels are created spirits, without bodies, having understanding and free will.

--BALTIMORE CATECHISM, NO 3, LESSON 4

Angels can fly because they take themselves lightly.

--G.K. CHESTERTON

From dust you came, and to dust thou shalt return.

--LENTEN INJUNCTION TAKEN FROM GENESIS 3:19

Chapter One

Spark: Are you here yet? Are you in communication? Reply, please.

Log Entry: M. Lamb: No reply. Odd. While I await my associate's response, I shall record my impressions and locate my subject.

As usual, manifestation was a shock, even for a veteran like me. One leaps in a twinkling from ether to lead, from light to shadows, from thrones and dominions to footstools and clay. How odd to mutate from pure spirit to human dust! How, I wonder, did the One who is our heart endure so sluggish and awkward a machine for thirty-three years!

Yet here I am, tumbled into a crowd in Pritchard Park in Asheville, North Carolina. The time is 6:56 Eastern Standard Time. The date is Friday, May 16, 2014. According to the Seraphic Manuel 35.1, materializing in a swarm of people is the preferred means of entry, as it diminishes the flash-and-bang of scaring some poor human soul witless.

When making my appearance, I sound the traditional alarm, "Be not afraid," but no one pays me the slightest attention except the dark-haired child at my elbow, a boy three or four years of age, who glances up, recognizes, as small children are wont to do, my true nature, and chirps, "Okay." His mother, who sees him speaking to me, puts her hand round his shoulder, bends to his ear, and mutters a warning about talking to strangers. When the boy keeps smiling at me, she interposes her body between us and sidles away.

This human congregation into which mother and child disappear has gathered this warm and pleasant evening for a strange ritual called a "drum circle." These drums and the accompanying dance remind me of a week I spent in the Congo in 1885, when brutal Belgium overlords worked the natives to death. The Lokele people in those dark days communicated with one another using bongungus, signaling their lamentations and despair by drum, most often at dawn.

Their drums throbbed with a harrowing beauty: this present entertainment is an ugly charade. Fifty feet from me, some twenty drummers sit side by side on concrete benches, beating out repetitious rhythms on hand-held drums. Ranging from teens to the geriatric, these bucket-beaters pound away on a variety of thud-boxes, some constructed from steel, some from plastic, some from the tanned hides of animals. Before them on the flat courtyard of the park some thirty dancers, mostly female, stomp their feet to the monotonous rhythm, swirling, swaying, their arms undulating like serpents. Several hundred observers surround these drummers and dancers, some of them clapping their hands or nodding to the primitive beat, others clicking away with their cameras like anthropologists among savages. This hot arena smells of automobile fumes, marijuana, body odor, and traces of vomit and urine.

From time to time one of the female dancers raises her head toward the heavens and ululates like an Arab. Her cry brings to mind another of my assignments, when, dispatched so very long ago to offer hope to an Italian slave in Damascus, I watched warriors in their white thobes and checked ghutras ride from the city on prancing stallions and groaning camels, waving their swords and promising death to their enemies. The dancer's cries bring back the memory of women standing on the walls and roofs of that city, uttering their own ululations of grief and harsh exhortation.

As I make my way through the crowd, I pause to observe one of the dancers, an extraordinarily tall human I initially take to be female. Closer examination reveals the shadow of a beard and masculine facial features, both of which dictate against the breasts and skirt of the creature. "A transvestite," I murmur aloud.

I clearly speak more loudly than I intended, for a bare-footed woman with tangled dreadlocks stops caressing the shoulder of her teenage companion, turns to me, swears, and with disgust adds, "Get it right, asshole. That's Ursula, and she's transgendered. A transvestite wears the clothes of the opposite sex, but Ursula's had the fucking operations."

"Operations?" I say. "You mean those breasts aren't original? And the nether-parts are—"

"Oh, for God's sakes," the woman says. She swears at me again, and then addresses the girl, who stares glassy-eyed in my direction. "Come on, baby. Let's dance."

For God's sake indeed.

Spark: Are you there? Is something wrong? You're late, you know. Respond!

Log Entry: M. Lamb: Still no response. Very unusual.

As the two daughters of Lesbos attach themselves to the thumping drumbeats, I spot my contact on the far side of the crowd. John Flyte is standing with two acquaintances beneath a sickly maple, watching the spectacle and punching away at his iPhone. Let it be recorded that he is wearing a baseball hat turned backwards, a T-shirt sporting some sort of logo, a pair of baggy shorts, and running shoes, an outfit pronouncing him more boy than man. His adolescent garb dismays me: it can only make our work more difficult. Let us pray the young lady he is destined to meet has eyes for his physical appearance rather than for his clothing.

For John Flyte is, as I find when I edge around the crowd and come closer to him, a well-built specimen, thin, muscular, and just a tad under six feet. His hair is brown and cropped short; his eyes are dark, most likely brown; he is tanned, despite the season; his lean face is passably handsome. He gives me, in short, material suitable for work.

At this particular moment his face most attracts my attention. He stands slightly apart from his two companions, both slouching males, and though he participates in their talk and laughter—he has returned his phone to his pocket—that sharp-cut face reflects an inner anxiety, a perplexity with the world and his place in it. His history, given me during my briefing, reveals a lack of faith in anything beyond the material world, yet like most of his race John Flyte is haunted by that nagging sensation of a realm beyond this veil of tears, some place better than the world in which he dwells, a home beyond home.

Each time I embark on a manifestation, I am both fascinated and baffled by this longing among human creatures for their real home. They feel the longing, but they disbelieve in its reality, and so they attempt to fill the void inside themselves in a thousand ways other than seeking the Way. They strive to satisfy that desire, that interior emptiness eating away at them, with all sorts of philosophies, some of them noble, some inane, some as cracked as a broken dish, and to mask their discontent, they chase a rainbow of pleasures—money, drink, sex, sports, hobbies. They make for themselves a thousand tiny gods that bring, predictably, tiny satisfactions.

Our young man, John Flyte, and his friends have turned from the park and are crossing the street. I am in pursuit and will notify my partner of their whereabouts in another quarter hour.

Spark: Have you arrived? Are you all right? Have you located your subject? Where in heaven's name are you?

Spark: Oww! Owwwwww!

Spark: Oww? What do you mean?

Spark: It hurts.

Spark: What hurts?

Spark: Manifestation hurts. And the controller manifested me next to a rose bush and my wrist was caught on the thorns.

Spark: Of course manifestation hurts. Surely you remembered that?

Spark: How could I remember?

Spark: Oh, no. No, no, no.

Spark: I feel all wobbly inside.

Spark: Please. Please tell me you have manifested on previous occasions. Please tell me you are a veteran.

Spark: I am Novice Class, Yellow Rank.

Spark: YELLOW RANK? YELLOW RANK? Repeat, please!

Spark: I am Novice Class, Yellow Rank.

Spark: In the name of all the angels and saints, what are you doing here?

Spark: I was dispatched.

Spark: We should have trained together.

Spark: My controller refused training me with you.

Spark: WHAT?

Spark: My controller said our mission was special and you were accustomed to coping with the unknown.

Spark: Why me? Why now?

Spark: For heaven's sakes!

Spark: Very amusing. All right, then. I can work with any material, however inept or clumsy.

Spark: I didn't know we were allowed to be snarky.

Spark: Mark it down to my assigned human personality. And I do feel snarky. Thunderously so. Now, where are you?

Spark: I was manifested behind a privet bush in the garden of an apartment building on Cumberland Avenue.

Spark: Have you managed to liberate yourself from the deadly rose bush?

Spark: Yes. And there's no need for sarcasm. Why on earth do humans find this bush of thorns so romantic?

Spark: The beauty of its bloom, its scent, its intricate pattern, and possibly its prickly stem. Now to business: have you located your subject?

Spark: She just now walked past the garden.

Spark: If you have recovered from your wounds, I suggest following her.

Spark: I'm trying, but my feet and hands aren't operating properly.

Spark: Move, move, move! Your limbs will feel better with movement.

Spark: I'm spinning and I keep falling down.

Spark: Did they teach you nothing? Move!

Spark: I see her. She's about a block away, walking slowly.

Spark: Quickly, tell me your assigned name.

Spark: Hart. Mary Margaret Hart. I don't like it very much. Please, just call me Maggie.

Spark: My assigned name is Maximilian Lamb, Ms. Hart. My acquaintances here will call me Max, but you, Ms. Hart, will address me as Mr. Lamb in these sparks.

Log Entry: M. Hart: I had no idea we were allowed to be snits to each other. It must have to do with our human manifestations.

I am now walking slowly behind my contact toward town.

The heaviness of my form, the scents of flowers and mown grass, the sound of robins, crows, mockingbirds, and traffic, the touch of the breeze on my face: these sensations dizzy me. My limbs are functioning better, but my feet keep getting tangled up. I feel like a fourteen-year-old in heels.

Emily Hoffman is alone this evening, as she is alone most evenings, and is walking, as she often walks, the eight long blocks from her apartment to the Battery Park Book Exchange and Champagne Bar for a glass of chardonnay and some reading. She is wearing a yellow sundress and brown sandals, and carries a green shoulder bag for her purse. Her auburn-red hair falls to her shoulders, and is kept from her face and eyes with a yellow headband. Her glasses—black-rimmed, of all things!—detract from her good looks, but they do magnify, as I observed when she passed me, a pair of beautiful eyes. Those eyes are her strongest feature: wide, blue as the heavens, guarded. She wears only a touch of makeup. She could use, I think, a little meat on her bones—she has a slight build and appears frail—but she has a lovely slim neck. Despite the fact that she teaches kindergarten at a local Montessori school, and so has her summers free, she apparently avoids the heat of the sun, for her skin is alabaster and lightly freckled. Her posture is a marvel, the result of ballet lessons taken through high school. She has no visible marks or piercings.

This particular evening, Emily wears an aura of dejection, of sadness. According to my sources, she travels many nights to the champagne bar, where many men have approached her, but always she has politely turned them away. Part of her rejection stems from her fear of the new. (You would think a kindergarten teacher would be accustomed to the new). Mostly, though, she is shy, protective of her heart, fearful of being hurt again.

Unlike Mr. Lamb's man, Emily is a believer, a communicant at the Basilica of Saint Lawrence, which the two of us will pass if she follows her regular path. I wish I could record that her faith was that of a lioness, but reports indicate she has lately questioned the Church's teaching, particularly in the areas of sexuality and of all things, euthanasia. Her grandmother died last Christmastide of pancreatic cancer in North Florida, and Emily now asks herself if she shouldn't have helped her die to avoid so much suffering.

It is not our role to question the purpose of Emily and John meeting each other, but I do wonder whether such an encounter might cause grave damage to her soul.

There: that is description as it should be, as I was so instructed to deliver.

One final note: having recorded my remarks about Emily's appearance, I wonder about my own. Am I by human standards pretty? I wonder if there is a mirror in my purse.

Spark: Where are you now, Ms. Hart? My contact is entering the Battery Park Book Exchange and Champagne Bar.

Log Entry: M. Lamb: John Flyte is approaching the bookstore alone. His two companions wanted to drink at the Bier Garden, a local sports bar, and teased him when he insisted on going first to the bookstore. "Come on, man," said the shorter friend, who has the build of a baseball catcher. "The Braves are playing." "Books?" said the other, taller and ruddy from the sun, and wearing a tattoo of a dragon on his forearm. "What kinda wuss are you?" "I like their Civil War collection," Flyte said, striding off toward the store and calling back over his shoulder that he would "catch you later."

Spark: Our progress is slow but assured. When setting foot on Flint Street, Emily stopped to pick a magnolia blossom from the sidewalk. Someone must have ripped the poor thing from the tree, only to discard it. She spent a full minute studying the branch and its blossom and then, carrying it with her, continued her procession uptown. She seems even more pensive. Not a good sign.

We are now passing the Basilica. In the Marian Garden Emily stopped before the statue of Our Lady and placed the magnolia blossom at her feet. How sweet. And there are lots of lightning bugs, as people here call them. They signal one another as do you and I, with flashes and sparks rather than words. Lovely little creatures....

Spark: I know what lightning bugs are. They also go by the more noble title of fireflies.

Spark: Still in a mood, are we?

Spark: I asked where you were and you responded with magnolia blossoms and bugs.

Spark: We're passing the Basilica. The church is throbbing with the light and power of the One located inside in the tabernacle. Oh Max, it's so beautiful.

Spark: Please, let's be professional, Ms. Hart.

Spark: My apologies, Mr. Lamb. A question. Can human beings see this energy of the One the way we can?

Spark: Most cannot. Too bound in the flesh. Too settled into the earth. Maybe a few of the saints. Now where are you?

Spark: We are within sight of the Grove Arcade, which of course contains the bookshop, and you have neglected to ask me about my appearance. Or was that on purpose?

Spark: I have a better question. How can you know your appearance?

Spark: I found a mirror in my shoulder purse and looked at myself.

Spark: Good grief! You took time to do that?

Spark: I wanted to see how the controller manifested me. I just wanted a peek. Max—I mean, Mr. Lamb—I think I am what human beings would describe as chubby.

Spark: What do you mean?

Spark: I mean, I think I'm about twenty pounds over the optimal weight.

Spark: That's not chubby. Women on Internet dating sites with extra pounds describe themselves as "curvy." Like Bridget Jones in the movies.

Spark: Who is Bridget Jones?

Spark: Look it up in Reference. Now

Spark: In case you're wondering, you will find me about Emily's height, 5'5" tall, but heavier. Hair: blonde tied in a braid, worn over my right shoulder. Eyes: hazel. Face: full. Attire: black dress but informal. Footwear: black sandals. Jewelry: A single slim gold necklace and a number of bands of different colors on my left forearm.

Do you remember Constantia? She accompanied you on a mission not long ago in human time to that house church in China. She told me that you sometimes neglected details. Please keep me apprised of your appearance.

One more thing: How should we approach them?

Spark: While you were mirror-gazing, we have arrived inside the store. My client has secured a glass of red wine—the cheapest in this establishment—and has gone off toward the coffee bar, now closed for the evening, and the shelves of books beyond. After asking for my own glass—I chose the house champagne, and am delighted by the effervescent tickling of my nose and upper lip—I followed in his trail and have found him grazing a long shelf of war histories. He seems, like so many of his gender, particularly smitten with the accounts of violence and mayhem in which human beings so often indulge. I have settled near him in the gardening books and am currently perusing a volume detailing the rudiments of growing radishes.

As for Constantia! I well remember her. The controllers manifested her as a young woman grieving from a forced abortion and seeking solace in the church. An easy role to play: she had merely to shed tears and the congregants—a non-denominational sect of Bible believers—warmed her with pity. I had the onerous task of being a Marxist student confused about God. Try on that part for size, and then critique me for absent-mindedness.

Spark: Mr. Lamb, I meant no disrespect. I—

Spark: A quick note on my appearance. Height: 6'. Weight: about 180 lbs. Face: pleasant, angular, and intense. Hair: black. Eyes: dark brown. Clothing: white shirt with sleeves rolled up on the forearm, khaki trousers, shoes but no socks. I resemble what might be charitably called a "prep or preppie." No scars or visible marks. No jewelry. No accouterments of any kind save the billfold in the hip pocket of my trousers and the sunglasses in the pocket of my shirt.

Incidentally, I discerned these details with a glance at my reflection in a store window. Please, put away the mirror.

Now, contact me immediately on your entrance, and we will lay our plans.

Spark: My regrets for having offended you. Please mark my comments as stress-induced. Constantia never mentioned the characters the two of you played. Charity demands that she misapprehended your difficulties.

We have arrived, and Emily Hoffman is approaching the wine bar. Ideas for our relationship? Brother and loving sister?

Spark: No, no. We can't pass as siblings. You don't resemble me in the least, either in appearance or, I suspect, in demeanor. We will employ the friendship gambit. We met each other at the University of Virginia. You graduated with a degree in nursing and presently work at Mission Hospital. I am an attorney in Winston-Salem who has traveled to the mountains to visit you. I am also investigating the possibility of moving my practice here. You approach Emily, I John, and when he appears comfortable I will bring him to meet you. This tactic will preclude your client's propensity to flee from male advances.

I do wish John Flyte would either remove or front that baseball cap. Right now he is examining a book on the Boer War, and with the backwards cap, his parted lips, and the blank look on his face, he could serve as a breathing billboard for witless nincompoops.

Spark me when you have news.

Spark: You are awfully rough in your description of John Flyte.

Spark: You are correct. I apologize to nincompoops everywhere.

Spark: At the bar, Emily ordered a New Zealand chardonnay, also the cheapest wine in the establishment, and a glass of water. For myself I selected a German white, expensive but I simply couldn't resist. How strange everything is! I spoke my first words to a barmaid with a tattoo of an anchor on her shoulder, its chains running up her throat. When I sipped my wine, I choked and coughed, but the second sip glided down my esophagus and took some of the evening's heat from my face.

Emily has poured some of the water into the wine, no doubt to increase the longevity of the glass. She then dilly-dallied in poetry for a moment—she opened a volume of Hopkins, a good sign—and is now perusing the shelves of fiction in the room just down the steps from you. If you turn, you'll see her. She has deposited her glasses of wine and water on the short table, and is currently flipping the pages of Tender Is The Night.

Should we switch to client-history modality?

Spark: Commence client-history modality.

Public File: Client History: John Flyte

"The Boer War. Have you read Churchill's account of the skirmish at the train?"

"Pardon me," John says, startled by my intrusion.

Approaching strangers in this country and era is uncommon, and John Flyte regards me warily. I observe that the brown eyes are flecked with green. Another note: he's missed a spot shaving that morning, right below his left nostril. I wonder if Emily Hoffman will notice his negligence.

When he remains silent—perhaps he thinks I'm hitting on him for money or sex—I repeat, "Churchill. Have you read him?"

My voice, controlled, deep, with just a twist of that bored sophistication of a BBC commentator, pleases me. I hadn't remarked its cool timbre at the drum circle. "During the Boer War, Churchill was captured during a fight at a train and hauled off to prison. Later he escaped, miraculously found refuge with the only English sympathizer within a hundred miles, spent several days hiding in a cave with albino rats, and eventually returned to England as a hero. The Brits needed a hero then—the war wasn't going particularly well."

As usual, radiating trust, empathy, and love through human flesh initially proves a challenge. I modulate my voice, smile, and look him in the eye with interest but not intensity.

"I've never heard that story," John says. He has a firm voice himself, pleasant, a trifle flat with a slight low-country drawl. He wears caution like a buckler. He's still sporting the baseball hat, which bears the logo of the Braves, and he looks like a big goofy kid. The self-doubt I had earlier witnessed in him, the questions, are not evident in that voice, but vestiges remain on his face, the chronic despondency of the unbeliever. "I don't really know much about the Boer War."

"I dabble a bit in military history. I'm actually more interested in the Civil War."

"Hey, me too. That and World War II."

"Four things greater than all things are: women and horses and power and war."

He gapes at me like a yokel, his mouth hanging open.

"Kipling," I explain.

"Oh, that English guy. *The Jungle Book?*"

I nod. "That English guy."

He slips the book into its place on the shelf. "Have you read Foote's trilogy on the Civil War?"

"I have. A fine piece of work. What did someone call it? The American Iliad?"

Two women and a man, carrying long-stemmed glasses and a bottle of champagne, push past us on their way to the stairs, and we move into one of the nearby sitting areas. This shop truly is extraordinary, with its high ceilings, the wine and champagne bar, shelves and shelves of secondhand books, the scattering of plump chairs and sofas.

"Yeah, I read that quote somewhere myself. I got hooked on Foote when I watched him on the Ken Burns Civil War documentary. Have you seen that?"

"No, I've only read the books."

"All that Southern charm. I could have listened to him for hours. Heck, Foote could've made a living on television."

"But then we might not have the books."

"True." A question poised itself on his face, and then he made his decision and stuck out his right hand. "I'm John, by the way. John Flyte."

"Maximilian Lamb," I say, shaking his hand. He has a good grip. "Please, call me Max."

"You have an interesting accent. English?"

"A boyhood in London. My father died before I really knew him. Heart failure. My mother was a brilliant woman, much brighter than I, and she worked in corporate law in London for Debevoise and Plimpton. I was back in the States and in law school at the University of Virginia when she fell ill and died. Right now I'm living in Winston-Salem."

Always my motto during manifestation: Keep the biography simple and get the details out of the box right from the start. That modus operandi has always worked for me.

"How about you? Are you native to Asheville?"

Of course I know he's from the Coast. The files on him are quite complete.

"Wilmington."

"You must miss the sand and surf."

"Sometimes. But I get back home three or four times a year."

That isn't quite the truth. In the past two years, John has trotted down to the Coast quite a bit, not to Wilmington but to Emerald Isle, where his paramour, now his former paramour, works for a real-estate company. Their falling-out in January turned nasty, doubtless one more of the reasons his damaged soul lacks love. For almost a year this woman had filled some of the gap in his heart, a gap now yawning into a crevasse.

"What brought you to the mountains?"

"Well, I went to pharmaceutical school in Chapel Hill, but I did my undergraduate work at the university here, and even then I decided I wanted to come back to Asheville someday. It's a great town with lots to do, and I sure don't miss the summers in Wilmington. And you? What sort of law do you practice?"

"General. Some light criminal. A little real estate." I gesture toward the shelves around us. "This is an absolutely magnificent bookstore. Is it always so crowded?"

"I think so, but I'm only here on the weekends." John looks around the store. "I like coming here. It takes my mind off things."

"Good wine and good books—I can see how it would."

His face comes back to mine. "I've heard it's tough finding work as an attorney these days."

"I'm doing all right."

"What brings you to Asheville?"

"An old friend from university days. She lives here now. I popped up for a visit and to look at some property. She's here somewhere. Why don't you come along and say hello? I'm sure Maggie would enjoy meeting you."

Public File: Client History: Emily Hoffman

My approach is gentle. Emily is a shy soul, comfortable only around her students.

She shelves the Fitzgerald book and settles onto a chair near the front window. She chooses this spot deliberately, I suspect, as a bookcase hides her from customers coming from the bar. From her purse she pulls Susan Howatch's *The High Flyer.* Literarily speaking, Howatch is a cut above the Christian books Emily normally reads, and I wonder if the tangle of theology and sex in these novels may not reflect Emily's own inner turmoil.

I pretend to examine the shelves of fiction near her. Finally I am standing beside her. "Oh, you're reading Howatch," I remark, and the sound of my voice surprises both of us, Emily because I am speaking to her, me because I am startled, as I was when ordering my wine, by a sort of merry air this voice provides my words, as if, when I speak, I am suggesting a great adventure to my listener.

Emily turns her face to me. Again I notice the smattering of freckles on her nose and upper cheeks, and find them endearing. I wonder what John Flyte thinks of freckles. If only Emily would remove those glasses and try smiling, she would be lovely.

"Susan Howatch," I say, pointing toward Emily's book. "I've read all of her Church of England novels. What do you think so far?"

She lays the novel in her lap, keeping her eyes on me, and fumbles for her glass of wine, nearly spilling it. "I like the old priest best, Father Darrow. You know, the mystic? And the gruff priest. Lewis."

"I remember Father Darrow well," I say. Heavens, how could I forget him? I've heard tales of dozens like Darrow over the centuries, souls as in tune with the Creator as we are. "And his son Nicholas. I like him, too."

"You're one of the few people I've ever met who's even heard of these books. Did you read her earlier ones? The big best-sellers?"

"No, I'm afraid not."

"They're good, too, but not as good as this Church series. I would love to talk to her and see what made her write them."

"Well, she clearly has an interest in spiritual matters."

"Yes, she does. And she really shows the reader how the Anglican Church is breaking apart. How it's splintered, I mean."

"Has it splintered?" Of course, I know that the poor old church has splintered, smashed by the shoals of heresy and the ugly desire to be perceived as nice rather than faithful, but I want to keep her talking.

"Oh, yes. It's all broken up. And not just the Anglicans." She looks away from me, as if frightened by any possible disagreement on my part. "Most churches are in the same fix. They try to please everyone and aim for inclusion, but they don't always understand truth and love."

"What do you mean?"

"That along with love you have to teach the truth."

"And what is truth?"

Emily smiles. A tiny sad smile, but it relieved the tension of her face. "Someone else once asked that question."

"Pontius Pilate. And he didn't get an answer to the question."

"Maybe because the answer was standing right in front of him." She pauses, making sure once again that she hasn't offended me. "Without that truth, love becomes meaningless."

Her shyness and earnest words give her an unexpected sweetness. She is one of those souls whose gentle ways draw prayers of protection from beyond this veil of tears, and I find myself liking her very much. "With a statement like that, I'm betting you're a teacher."

"Yes, but I teach—

I hold up one hand. "Don't tell me. Let me guess. Not college—I don't think you could survive the faculty meetings. Not high school—you don't, if you'll pardon my saying so, seem hardened enough. I don't see you teaching middle-school." (Middle-school students would eat her alive). "That leaves elementary school. Kindergarten?"

"That's amazing. You've guessed it exactly. I must be transparent."

"Sheer luck. I'm Margaret, by the way. Mary Margaret Hart."

She stands and shakes my outstretched hand. "Emily Hoffman." When she releases my hand, she says, "You don't hear Margaret much anymore."

"I go by Maggie most of the time."

"Well, how about you? What do you do? I won't try to follow your performance—I'm no good at guessing games."

"I'm a nurse," I say, and leave it at that. Unnecessary details can bring questions, or so I was taught, and questions lead to connections, which can spell trouble. "This is a wonderful shop, isn't it?"

She nods. "I come here a lot."

"It's my first time. I wanted to show Max around town."

"Max?

"A friend from my college days."

Between us falls an awkward pause. Emily's interest is fading. She's still smiling at me, but her eyes are wondering why I don't make my farewell. Where is Mr. Lamb? If he doesn't appear soon, I'll need to break contact, which is unacceptable, or else go on blithering. "Max is his name," I add. "He's in town for a visit. He's an attorney. Real-estate, wills, driving violations—he handles all that sort of stuff."

Where are you, Mr. Lamb? I spark him, one tiny burst of energy to signal my anxiety, just as he appears at my elbow, smiling at my impatience. John Flyte stands awkwardly behind him in his goofy baseball cap.

"Maggie, I'd like you to meet John Flyte."

Spark: You! You goose! Are you crazy! What did you mean putting your arm around my shoulders that way? Are you so thick that you don't know how human creatures interpret that gesture? I may be new to this game, but—

Spark: Manners, my dear Ms. Hart, manners. To assess a situation and to change tactics according to that assessment is Standard Operating Procedure.

Within seconds of the introductions, I sensed John Flyte being torn in his attractions between the two of you. Your client was his initial magnet—her hair color and shape fit his preconceptions of beauty—but his attention then seemed drawn to you, especially after you spoke. I must say the controller gave you an enchanting voice. And after all, your client, Emily, was wearing those horrid spectacles, and her eyes and her body language—she leaned away from him with her arms folded—dropped a portcullis clearly intended to deflect his further interest.

You, on the other hand: you have that melodious voice filled with—there is no other way to say it—sex. (What was your designer thinking?) Your dress was superior to Emily's, and seductive in its low-cut décolletage, and that gold necklace against your throat brought to mind the jeweled baubles women wear to emphasize naked vulnerability. It's too late now, of course, but your designer might do better during future manifestations to ditch the jewelry and fashion a dress less alluring.

And so I made a command decision and put my arm around you to indicate possession.

My gesture immediately marked off the territory available to him. John's interest turned again to Emily.

Surely you noticed?

With that explanation, let me suggest that you write our Post-Action Report. You need the practice. You may submit it to me first, if you like, and I shall comment if necessary.

Spark: Mr. Lamb, please forgive my outburst. You are correct. I failed to realize the effect of my appearance on John Flyte. As you also note, I am unused to dealing with matters of dress and jewelry. Your touch startled me, but now I realize your apprehensions regarding John. Please accept my deepest apologies.

I shall be glad to submit the Post-Action Report and will look forward to your critique.

Post-Action Report: M. Hart: The Meeting of Emily Hoffman and John Flyte

In our manifestations as Maximilian Lamb and Mary Margaret Hart, we introduced the clients at approximately 7:47 Eastern Standard time/United States/Earth.

Mr. Lamb introduced client John Flyte to me and then asked me to introduce him and John Flyte to Emily Hoffman. I introduced Emily as a kindergarten teacher and a reader; Mr. Lamb introduced his client as a pharmacist and lover of history. At this point John removed the baseball cap from his head, which demonstrates some propriety of upbringing. To dissuade John that I might be available to his affections, Mr. Lamb then put his right arm around my shoulders and said, "Maggie is the fiction lover. I pick up some histories and biographies from time to time, but I can't compare to her when it comes to reading. You know, I believe she has read every word F. Scott Fitzgerald ever wrote."

"I was just looking at *Tender Is The Night* a few minutes ago," Emily said. She turned to me. "I love Fitzgerald's writing." Then she blushed. "That sounds awfully banal, doesn't it? But I really do. Partly it's his writing and the way he expresses himself—he puts together such odd adjectives with nouns—and partly it's his romance with Zelda and their lives together. Once I visited their graves in Rockville."

"Really?" I said. That visit was not a part of her file. Maybe Emily was more a romantic than I had suspected.

"We had to read *Gatsby* in college," John remarked. "I'm not much on fiction, but I still remember that book. The ending—'beating against the current' and all that—stuck with me."

"And I," said Mr. Lamb, ruefully, "am outnumbered. I have never read *Gatsby* or anything else by Fitzgerald. I did read some of the work of Asheville's native son, Thomas Wolfe, before driving into the mountains."

John shook his head. "I tried Wolfe. Too many words."

Emily disagreed. "He was trying to capture it all. He failed, just the way Faulkner said, but he really wanted to put everything he had experienced on paper so that his readers could feel and think everything he'd seen and done."

"Faulkner," Mr. Lamb said. "I have read him. *The Sound and the Fury*—not for everyone, but brilliant. I don't know how the man ever kept the story together."

"And *Absalom, Absalom*," Emily said.

"Agreed," said Mr. Lamb.

"Have you read everything?" John was smiling at her when he asked the question. His smile noticeably widened when Emily removed those awful glasses and looked him directly in the face.

For the second time that evening her mouth flickered briefly into a smile, and she glowed a little, as if someone had turned on a lamp behind her face. “Not everything. But I do love the writers of the twenties and the thirties. I’ve read a lot of them.”

“Hemingway?” John asked her.

“Love him.”

“A woman after my own heart.”

She smiled again. I wondered if anyone other than me noticed the tiny blush at the base of her throat. “He was sometimes hard on women, but he made me fall in love with Paris.”

“You’ve gone to Paris?” Mr. Lamb asked. Like me, he at once realized this fact was missing from her file.

“Oh, no. No,” she added, more firmly. “*A Moveable Feast* made me fall in love with Paris. Someday I want to go.”

“You’ll love it,” John said.

“You’ve been there?”

“Twice. Once in college for a semester abroad program and again after graduation from pharmaceutical school.”

“Was it everything you wanted?”

“Whatever you’ve imagined Paris to be, you’ll find it there.”

“Did you visit Shakespeare and Company?”

“I did. The first time I went, George Whitman was still alive and running the shop.”

“Oh.” For a moment I thought Emily might actually put her hand over her heart.

Mr. Lamb removed his arm from my shoulder. “I could use a bite to eat. They offer cheese and bread platters here. Anyone else hungry? My treat.”

“It’s crowded,” John said. “I didn’t see any empty tables.”

“Then we’ll set up camp right here,” Mr. Lamb said. “You two ladies take the chairs. John, you keep everyone entertained while I fetch a cheese-board and a bottle of cabernet.”

“I can pay for the wine.”

"No, no, my treat," Mr. Lamb said. Though I could see we might have to square this expenditure later with accounting, Mr. Lamb was justified in the gesture. It would leave Emily and John that much more time to become acquainted.

Off he went to purchase the food and drink while the three of us chatted. His trip to the bar seemed to take forever, and I had to keep reminding myself that the pace of this world is much slower than our own. Eventually he returned, balancing the cheese-board in one hand, the bottle of cabernet in the other, napkins and cheese knife tucked into his shirt pocket.

"In case you're worried, the waitress says we needn't finish the wine. We can take the bottle with us." He put the plate and the wine on the low table and sat on the floor beside my chair. He was very cheerful. "Come on, John. Best seat in the house."

John sat awkwardly on the floor beside Emily's chair. Mr. Lamb sliced the cheese and took some bread. "Reminds me of a meal I once ate in Casablanca."

"You were in Casablanca?"

"Just for a short time." He poured wine for himself and John—Emily and I were still working on our drinks—and raised his glass for clicks all around. "To Asheville and new friendships."

I thought he was laying it on a little thick, but both Emily and John murmured the toast back at him, looked at each other, and drank.

"What else do you like to do besides reading?" John asked Emily.

"I volunteer at Hearts for Hands. I like contra dancing, but don't go very much. And walking."

"Hiking?"

Emily laughed. Her laughter surprised me. It was less guarded than her voice, light and musical. "I wouldn't call it that. More like strolling. You know, through town. How about you?"

"Racquetball at the Y. Lifting. Hiking. Movies. Video games." (Note for future reference: John Flyte's video games may indicate extended adolescence).

"Lifting?"

"Weights."

"Ah," Emily said.

"So. Are you originally from Asheville?"

"No, I grew up in Florida. Gainesville. But when I was in high school, our church youth group came on a mission trip here, and I fell in love with the mountains. I still remember how everything felt that week—so green and cool."

And so it went. Mr. Lamb and I tried, of course, to converse as little as possible, leaving to them the available precious minutes to become acquainted. John Flyte became more animated, and did more of the talking than Emily Hoffman. Unfortunately, much of his dialogue was directed at himself. He explained why he had become a pharmacist—"the hours, the money, an interest in science, and a fascination with the effects of pharmaceuticals on the human body." He then discussed, to an annoying degree, the movies of Bruce Willis, and went on far too long about his favorite video game, *Call of Duty*. Had I been Emily, John would have bored me out of my wits.

But she leaned toward him, her knees nearly touching his shoulders, smiling and nodding at his enthusiasms. Is she so lonely that she finds even an adolescent narcissist fascinating? John is handsome, his voice contains an animated timbre, and he did in fact focus his attention on her. His despair regarding the eternal, more easily spotted by us than by his fellow creatures, lay hidden behind his smile and words. But if the goal of future meetings is romance and love, then Mr. Flyte will need to mend his ways. Emily can only nod so many times before her stiffened neck will require medical treatment.

The evening ended when Mr. Lamb covered a yawn and made mention of the long day. We were running another test, of course, seeking to determine whether Emily and John might wish to be left alone. But both of them stood when Mr. Lamb rose to his feet.

"This was fun," John said. "I'm glad to have met you all."

"Me, too," Emily said.

There was a brief pause in which I sensed that John wanted to ask Emily for her number, but in spite of his bluff personality, he is clearly a stick when it comes to women. He needs to put away his Gameboy, X-Box, or whatever he plays at home, and find out more about the opposite sex.

"This was fun," I said, and suppressed a sigh for what I was about to say next. "Tomorrow evening I'm taking Max to the Sky Bar. Do you know it?"

Both of them nodded. "I've never been there," Emily said, while John put in: "I've gone there a couple of times. It's super-nice at twilight."

Super-nice? John Flyte also needs lessons in elocution.

"Why don't you two come along?" Mr. Lamb said. "We could meet in the lobby by the elevator around eight."

The two of them looked at each other, obviously wanting to spend the next evening together but frightened to be first to accept Max's invitation.

"Tomorrow works for me," John said. "I'm free."

"I'll be there," Emily said.

And so the evening ended.

Post-Action Report: Comments: M. Lamb

I approve this report. The evening was generally a success. We have brought the creatures together, and they parted company on an affable note. Both of them should spend tomorrow with a mild sense of anticipation. Perhaps the seeds sown this evening will produce growth.

I must add that I hardly found John as enervating as Ms. Hart has suggested. Had he afforded more of the conversation to Emily, the evening would have been marked by long, periodic silences. She is a bashful creature, timid as a rabbit.

Spark: Thank you, Mr. Lamb, for your approval of the report. But did you really need to compare Emily to a rabbit?

Should the two of us meet for supper tomorrow evening before the gathering at the Sky Bar? We might then become more accustomed to our manifestations and make some plans. Do you enjoy the food of the Ganges? Mela's, a restaurant on Lexington Avenue, specializes in Indian fare.

Spark: For now, let us agree to disagree about the natures of Emily and John.

The food of the subcontinent does indeed appeal to me. Some time in Goa during my forty-seventh manifestation gave me a taste for their spices. Sixish?

Spark: Six it is.

Spark: Mr. Lamb?

Spark: Yes, Ms. Hart?

Spark: I know I am inexperienced, but I would like your respect. I was properly taught and trained, you know.

Spark: Training is all well and good, but our service here on battleground earth is very different from training.

Spark: I feel you're upset with me.

Spark: The personality of Maximilian Lamb bleeds into these sparks. Lamb can be abrupt.

Spark: May I ask about your experience?

Spark: My experience?

Spark: Your missions? Your manifestations?

Spark: A thumbnail sketch: For the past millennium—I won't go back before that—I have appeared a total of 415 times in various manifestations. My shortest visit was for three minutes, when I appeared as humans popularly perceive us, all light and sparkles with wings on my back, to console a child dying of influenza in the epidemic of 1918. My longest time in carne was for two months at the siege of Acre in 1291, when I was dispatched to serve as a servant to a Knights Templar who was faltering in his faith and whose example was necessary to bolster the morale of his comrades. We fell at the end at the siege when the fortress collapsed.

I have comforted the dying, brought hope to the hopeless, helped sinners become saints, tasted the salt of ten seas, seen a thousand sunsets, and touched the dewy grass of five hundred dawns. I have seen men and women commit horrible deeds without exhibiting an ounce of remorse. I have seen others of the species rise above the desires and pains of the flesh, and behave so heroically that it brought tears to my human eyes.

Spark: I respect your experience, Mr. Lamb. I will try to live up to your standards.

Spark: Thank you, Ms. Hart.

Spark: Here's what I don't understand. Emily Hoffman and John Flyte—they don't seem particularly good or particularly wicked. I am wondering why we are here.

Spark: There you go again, Ms. Hart. You have revealed yourself as an amateur. We don't know why we're here. Why we're here is irrelevant. It's not a part of our job description. Could we conjecture the reason? Of course. Perhaps if Emily doesn't fall in love with John she will drive her car into a bridge abutment or drink poison or become an alcoholic. Perhaps if John doesn't love Emily he will cause a brigade of women to distrust men. Perhaps their child will find the cure for certain cancers or become a priest who leads a brigade of souls to heaven.

Spark: Then why not just help everyone?

Spark: An intelligent question. Heaven does help everyone. And human beings were created to help one another. That they don't always seek our help or offer that help to one another is the result of sin, neglect, ignorance, and sloth. At any rate, our job is to assist the chosen few to whom we are assigned. And to do that, we need our rest. You've had a big day.

Spark: Yes, but I do have one more question, Mr. Lamb. I know I'm a few pounds overweight according to current American standards of female beauty, but I was wondering if I looked attractive in that black dress.

Spark: You looked wonderful.

Spark: That's not much of an answer.

Spark: It's the universal male response to such a question. No man in his right mind offers any other reply.

Spark: But I want to know. Did the dress work okay for me? Did I look too heavy in black?

Spark: Are you there, Mr. Lamb?

Spark: Mr. Lamb?

Chapter Two

Public File: Discussion recorded: M. Hart and M. Lamb: Mela's Restaurant: Asheville

"Too hot for you?"

"The spices. They're making me sweat."

"Please, you're not sweating. You're glowing. Horses sweat, men perspire, and women glow."

"What are you talking about, Mr. Lamb?"

"It's a Victorian axiom of etiquette. As for the heat generated by the food, the source is the "Ghost Chili," red peppers whose fire is exacerbated by liberal doses of ginger."

"I need another glass of water. This chicken could scorch the Evil One's tongue."

"I'm sorry it doesn't agree with you."

"No, I love it. Really, Mr. Lamb. I want to taste everything I can. How do human beings stand this excitement every day?"

"Excitement?"

"These explosions in the mouth. Like last night when I bit into that pickle from the cheese tray. It puckered my lips and made an awful crunching sound, but the taste nearly caused me to moan with pleasure."

"You did moan with pleasure."

"Why are you smiling?"

"You amuse me. Few humans become excited over pickles."

"In the future, I will try to maintain control of myself."

"Please don't. You're amusing when you're amusing. And stop rolling your eyes. Only sixteen-year-olds do that."

"What's your favorite food?"

"Too many favorites to choose. Once when I was half-starved a bowl of Tom Yum Gung tasted heavenly."

"What's Tom Yum Gung?"

"It's a Thai soup—shrimp, mushrooms, tomatoes, lemongrass, galangal, and kaffir lime leaves. Add some coconut milk and the taste is exquisite."

"What was the worst?"

"A cold espresso served to me by an old woman in black in Palermo. It had the consistency of thin mud and kept me awake for twenty-four hours."

"Yuck."

"Yes."

"Should we talk about Emily and John now?"

"Oh, yes, the contacts."

"Do we have to refer to them as 'the contacts?'"

"What would you prefer, Ms. Hart?"

"How about Emily and John?"

"Sentimental, but this is your first adventure. Here are my thoughts. I suggest we arrive fashionably late for our appointment with them at the Sky Bar. Therefore, we may eat slowly. We may even order the dessert. Perhaps some pastries. Or fried bananas. These were quite good when I ate them in Goa a few centuries back."

"I see what you're getting at. If we arrive late, Emily and John will be forced into conversation with each other. What do you think? Five minutes?"

"Ten is even better."

"I wish we knew the final objective of this exercise."

"Well, we don't. And we won't. All we have to worry about is bringing them together."

"Right now I'm more concerned about us than them."

"Us?"

"What are we to be now that you've gone and draped your arm around me?"

"Clearly we must devise a new plan of attack. We should, I suppose, follow the template for romance."

"Is that done?"

"Were you not taught the templates?"

"Yes. But we were told that romance was rarely a useful tool. And wasn't that template designed for action between one of us and one of them?"

"Yes, but it might be effective in this particular case. The contacts—Emily and John, that is—might be inspired to emulate our behavior."

"We'd serve as their example?"

"Yes."

"Couldn't that be dangerous?"

"Our work is always dangerous."

"But what if we send them down the wrong path? Make John and Emily lovers before they know real love?"

"There is that risk. We'd have to walk a narrow rope. Still, it's worked in other instances. Once a good while back I was on a case in Normandy where emulation worked like a charm. I led the couple through a dance all the way to the altar."

"What year was that in human time?"

"The 1050s. The exact year escapes me—no one then seemed as keen on dates as they do now. My client was a man the world later knew as William the Conqueror, but who at the time bore the unfortunate name of William the Bastard because of the circumstances of his birth. At any rate, he wanted to marry Matilda of Flanders. When Matilda refused, telling him she could never marry a bastard, he caught up with her on her way to wed another, grabbed her by her braids, and flung her to the ground in front of her bridesmaids."

"How awful."

"Awful, yes, to most of us, but Matilda became quite smitten with him. She refused to marry anyone else, bore him nine or ten children, became a beloved queen, and held his affection until her death. The two of them made a striking couple. She was very short, much shorter than you, and he was well over six feet."

"And how did you assist them?"

"I joined William's household as a wandering knight. My steed impressed William—he had a keen eye for horseflesh—and I made him a gift of the beast. I then wooed Gwenaelle, a lady-in-waiting in Matilda's entourage. I treated Gwenaelle with gallantry and courtesy, and so impressed Matilda, who knew I was one of William's men. I also filled Gwenaelle's ear with the legends even then surrounding William and predicted he would one day be a king, meaning, of course, that his consort would be a queen. This woman carried my tales to her lady. Given her reaction to his violent courtship, Matilda was, I think, particularly impressed by William's brute strength."

"To what end?"

"Pardon?"

"What was the goal?"

"I have no idea. As you well know, we're never informed of the reason behind our mission. William conquered England, of course, but I'm not sure that was part of our plan. Lanfranc, William's nominee as the Archbishop of Canterbury, brought reform and good works to the Church. So perhaps that was the reason. Whatever the case, the template worked."

"I can't see John dragging Emily around by the hair."

"Nor I. More water?"

"Please."

"We can't be concerned with the ultimate goal of our mission. We're here for one reason: to bring Emily Hoffman and John Flyte together."

"I'm still not sure about serving as an example to them. Our manifestations are very different, you know."

"Explain, please."

"Well, I'm young and sort of loose and easy-going, and I admit, incredibly naïve. You are   "

"A little older?"

"Well, that. And formal. And you're very handsome, and I'm overweight."

"Like many women, you are too hard on yourself. You possess many attractive qualities."

"Really?

"Yes. Really."

"Tell me what you find attractive in me."

"I will do no such thing."

"Aw, come on."

"Never."

Why not?"

"For one, you won't remember the compliments. You'll remember only the omissions and worry over them like a loose tooth. For another, there is no need. Such compliments would contribute nothing to our mission."

"Back to us and the mission then?"

"Yes."

"All right. The differences between us. You're—well, you're—I don't know how to say it."

"Snitty?"

"More like snobby."

"Me? A snob? A snob is a parvenu, a pretender."

"All right. You're stuck-up."

"I think Maximilian Lamb is supposed to be somewhat supercilious."

"So it's not you? It's Mr. Lamb? You're really very humble?"

"How could one of us be supercilious?

"You like that word, don't you?"

"It does roll off the tongue."

"But saying supercilious makes you sound supercilious."

"You mistake snobbery for sophistication."

"Which brings me back to my original point. Aren't we an unlikely couple?"

"Not at all. You admire me for my worldliness and I admire you for your giddy innocence."

"I deny being giddy."

"You are the epitome of giddy. And stop rolling your eyes. Now, the fact is that John and Emily already perceive us as a couple. What we must do is try to lead them by example into a courtship."

"That may be difficult. John is going to require a major overhaul. He doesn't seem to know much about women. To be frank, he strikes me as something of a boob, like a lot of his gender."

"You're critical of him because he's male?"

"I beg your pardon. Do you really regard me as that unprofessional?"

"He clearly annoys you."

"That's unfair. What he has done—or really, what he hasn't done—with his life annoys me."

"Let's face it, Ms. Hart—your Emily isn't exactly the sweetest catch in the sea."

"Your metaphor fails you. Fish aren't sweet."

"Gates of Heaven! Let's stick to business."

"All right, then. You're proposing we concoct a romance between us. We set the example and hope they follow it."

"Precisely. I—what are you doing now?"

"You had a bit of sauce on the corner of your lip. I was removing it. What would they think of me?"

"Of you?"

"Of me. What would they think if I let my boyfriend walk around wearing a moustache of sauce?"

"Boyfriend sounds silly. I'm thirty-two years old."

"I prefer boyfriend to significant other."

"English is a marvelous tool, but I must admit the language is limited in this realm of description."

"Anyway, the sauce is gone. You're back to your old handsome self."

"It's a wonder that napalm didn't burn its way through my lips to my teeth. Do I look okay, by the way? Handsome, as you say?"

"By human standards, yes, you do indeed. That shirt looks good on you."

"You wouldn't break any mirrors yourself, Ms. Hart."

"If that's your idea of sweet-talking a girl, it won't fetch."

"I'll keep that in mind. We'll need to hold hands when we're around them."

"I suppose so."

"Several levels of affection are probably in order. Holding hands, teasing with the eyes, bumping hips—"

"Bumping hips? What do you mean?"

"You know. Playfully bumping hips if we happen to stand next to each other."

"I have no idea what you're talking about. And kissing—"

"Of course, we'll need to kiss, though I must tell you I haven't kissed in a month of manifestations. My most recent manifestations were generally to the sick or the dying, or to people who needed bucking up in one form or another. I did appear about twenty years ago to a pregnant fifteen year old, but she was much past the kissing stage. Her boyfriend had dumped her."

"Kissing—I don't know how."

"We put our lips together and make a puckering sound."

"Maximilian Lamb, romantic."

"At least I have kissed and been kissed. You are a total innocent."

"We are very different, Mr. Lamb."

"Ah, well. At least our names dance well together."

"Max and Maggie. Maggie and Max. Yes, that has some poetry to it."

"Maggie. Lots of poetry in that name alone. Lots of rhyming words, too. Waggy. Baggy. Naggy. Saggy. Hag—Ouch!"

Log Entry: M. Lamb: Splendid, splendid, splendid

Though our late arrival plan worried me—Emily and John might have exhausted themselves in those ten minutes alone with bungled words and galling silence—the tactic in fact worked its magic. Who would have guessed that in those few minutes they would discover a mutual affection for the music of Cole Porter, which surely marks them as rare among their generation? And from there they plunged into other shared interests: both enjoy water sports (he kayaking, she swimming); both disliked high school but came into their own in college; both ranked shrimp as a favorite food and agreed that the best Mexican food in town could be found at Papa's & Beer.

After we joined them and took the elevator to the Sky Bar, which is outdoors, they have engaged each other through conversation and laughter. John's ball cap is gone—he has clearly decked himself out for the evening—and Emily has gotten rid of those dreadful spectacles. Over the last hour or so, they have connected with each other. They have begun to cast about themselves that circle of exclusivity that—

Spark: Oh, Max, isn't it lovely up here in the Sky Bar? What a wonderful idea! Here we are high above Asheville, and the lights are twinkling against the hills and here's this splendid breeze and all the people around us laughing and having so much fun.

Spark: I'm in the middle of a log entry!

Spark: Look, Max—you can see right down into those condominiums. Look—there's a couple putting together their supper. That's so sweet, though I don't know if I'd want people staring into my kitchen. And look—in the apartment next to them there's that large man—I don't want to call him fat, I don't want to hurt anyone ever, but he does drip out over his chair—and he's watching television.

Spark: Didn't you hear me? I said I was—

Spark: And what about Emily and John? They adore each other, don't you think? Don't you think it's lovely, Max?

Spark: Remember the proprieties, Ms. Hart. In open conversation I am Max. In our private communications I am Mr. Lamb.

Spark: Oh, Max. I can't call you Mr. Lamb. Not on a night as beautiful as this one. You know, your name is cute in an ironical sort of way. You're anything but a lamb. You're more like a stuffy old owl. You know what I think?

Spark: What I think is that if you sit any closer to me you'll be in my lap. And you need to release my hand. My fingers are falling asleep. Here—let's stand for a moment and stretch our legs.

Spark: I think you're awfully cute, Max. And your hand feels so lovely. No wonder human beings like to hold hands. Do you remember yesterday how awkward I felt in my manifestation? I think I'm past that now. I don't feel heavy anymore. I feel lovely. Light as gossamer, light as a feather—that's me. Being up here with you makes me feel as if I'm just floating. The music out here is divine, don't you think? And this sangria is nectar on the tongue. No wonder human beings enjoy drinking.

Spark: You need to be careful. How much sangria have you imbibed, by the way? And stop speaking in clichés.

Spark: Do you think I'm pretty, Max?

Spark: For the love of all that's holy, focus on the clients. You're drifting.

Spark: Well, do you, Max? Do you? Do you think I'm pretty?

Spark: I already told you that at supper. And stop wiggling so much.

Spark: I'm practicing my hip bumps.

Spark: Desist now, Ms. Hart! You practically knocked me over the rail! And look—I've spilled part of my martini.

Spark: Oh, Max. Max, Max, Max. Do you have to be so stuffy? Let yourself go. Look at John and Emily. Aren't they lovely? Look how closely John's bent his face toward hers. And she's so shy and sweet. Aren't they lovely?

Spark: Exactly how many glasses of sangria have you put away?

Spark: Your manifestation is in wonderful shape, Max. You must work out at a gym. Your biceps are very powerful. Do you like my dress?

Spark: By the portals of eternity, did you just nibble my ear?

Recording file: Voice-activated identification: Maximilian/ Recorder on

John: Flyte's an English name. My mother's ancestors were mostly Scotch-Irish, English, and one Frenchman thrown in from the continent. How about Hoffman?

Emily: German. There's English and German in my family. That's as far as I know. How about you, Margaret?

Maggie: Please—Maggie.

Emily: Maggie.

Maggie: Oh, let's ask Max. What am I, Max? Can you tell them what I am?

Max: Right now you are a young lady with too many sangrias under her belt.

Maggie: Oh, pooh.

Max: Pooh?

Maggie: As in Winnie-the-Pooh. Hey, where did that name come from? Why would a bear be named Pooh? And isn't Winnie a woman's name?

Emily: The name came from Christopher Milne, the author's son. Pooh was originally the name of a pet swan. And Winnie, Christopher insisted, was a male bear.

Maggie: You're so smart, Emily. How'd you know that?

Emily: I teach kindergarten.

Maggie: Yes, yes, so you do. And I'll bet you're a great teacher. Don't you think Emily's a great teacher, John?

John (laughing): I'm sure she's very good.

Maggie: No, she's great. And lovely, too. Isn't Emily lovely, John?

John (more laughter): Yes, she's lovely too, Maggie.

Max: Well, now that we've settled that—

Maggie: And you're lovely, too, Max. So lovely. You don't mind if I kiss you, do you?

Max: I don't think—.

Max: Well, I guess it doesn't matter whether I mind or not.

Maggie: Don't you just love it up here? Isn't it lovely? The lights and the people are all just lovely. Everything is so lovely.

Max: I need to buy you a thesaurus.

John: Do you go much to the Arboretum, Emily?

Emily: No. I keep meaning to buy a pass.

John: I know we've just met and everything, and I've already taken up your Saturday evening, but I was wondering if you'd like to come with me to the Arboretum tomorrow.

Emily: I'd love to.

Max: No more kissing, my dear. And no more juice either.

Maggie: Then I'll just lay my head on your shoulder. I'm feeling awfully lazy and sleepy right now.

Max: I'm sure you are.

Maggie: Did you say we're going to the Arboretum tomorrow, John?

John: Well, I was thinking that Emily and I—

Maggie: We'd love to go, wouldn't we, Max? All those trees and flowers. I just love the outdoors. Don't you, Emily? Don't you just love the outdoors?

Emily: Yes.

Max: Aren't we busy tomorrow? Tennis, wasn't it?

Maggie: Oh pish-posh on the tennis. We can play tennis any old time. A picnic sounds lovely.

John: I was thinking that—

Maggie: Sunday in the park. Sandwiches and pickles, chips and apple slices. Maybe we should bring a canteen of sangria. These are lovely drinks, aren't they, Max?

Max: Lovely, indeed. Now close your eyes. There—that's the way. She's never like this, you know. Perhaps it's the altitude.

Maggie: Closing my eyes doesn't make me deaf.

John: It's probably time to go anyway. Emily, you said you walked here. Can I give you a lift?

Emily: Thank you. That would be nice.

John: Max, Maggie, good to see you this evening.

Max: And you. Tomorrow at one all right?

John: Sounds good. Let's meet in the parking lot.

Maggie: I want to give Emily a hug. Oops.

Max: There, there, my dear. Keep your feet and stay away from the rail. I think we'll just settle here for a bit longer. Good night, you two.

Emily: Good night.

John: Good night.

Max: They're gone. You may now release my hand.

Maggie: But it feels so nice.

The sound of a lighter striking.

Maggie: What are you doing? I didn't know you smoked.

Max: Apparently I do. These were in the pocket of my jacket this evening. American Spirit Lights. Nice. (The sound of a long exhalation).

Maggie: Let me try one, Max.

Max: If our guides had wanted you to smoke, they'd have given you cigarettes.

Maggie: Oh, come on, Max. Don't be a stuffy old owl. Let me try one.

Max: It's unwise.

Maggie: Come on, Max. Please? I'll stop holding your hand if you let me try.

The sound of a lighter striking.

The sound of violent coughing.

Recording file from Saturday evening sent to Mary Margaret Hart.

Recording file immediately deleted by Maximilian Lamb after transmitting to Mary Margaret Hart.

After-Action Report: M. Lamb

We met the contacts, Emily Hoffman and John Flyte, outside the elevators of the Flat-Iron Building. Because of our deliberate delay, we arrived sixteen minutes late for our meeting. Our strategy worked as planned; Emily and John were chatting amiably—perhaps even more than amiably—when we met them in the lobby. We took the elevator, operated by a young man, to the Sky Bar and found an outside table on the patio overlooking the city.

In the Sky Bar the contacts continued their conversation, assisted as needed by us. They compared notes about their childhood—I noted that John was reluctant to give more than basic information—their experiences in college and in travel, restaurants they enjoyed in Asheville, and various other topics. At the end of the evening John asked Emily to come with him the following day to the Arboretum. Ms. Hart and I will accompany them on this outing.

I rate this evening highly successful.

Chapter Three

Spark: Hi.

Spark: Feeling a little subdued this morning, are we?

Spark: Mr. Lamb, I'm so sorry.

Spark: I know.

Spark: Truly, truly sorry. I don't know what got into me.

Spark: A pitcher or so of sangria.

Spark: My apologies, Maggie. I shouldn't have said that. It was uncharitable. Please communicate with me.

Spark: You called me Maggie.

Spark: Yes. In vino, veritas. You were right about me and right to call me out. I was being stuffy. A stuffy old owl.

Spark: I'm sorry, Mr. Lamb. So sorry. The report you sent to me—

Spark: Only went to you. I deleted the recording file after forwarding it to you. You're the sole possessor. And please call me Max.

Spark: Thank you, Max, so much. But He'll know. He knows.

Spark: He will and He does. And He will, I am certain, forgive you your indulgence. It wasn't intentional. You just aren't accustomed to the effects of alcohol on flesh.

Spark: That's an understatement at best. They warned us against the power of alcohol in training. I'm afraid sometimes I don't listen well. Anyway, I am sorry. I don't really have any excuse. It's just that we were up there on that rooftop and it was really beautiful—

Spark: Lovely, you mean.

Spark: You make me smile, Max. Lovely, then. Anyway, there we were at the top of that building and all the lights were coming out and the mountains and hills were so blue and John and Emily were sitting close together. Do you think human beings can see how beautiful the world is, Max?

Spark: Not very often.

Spark: And when I held your hand I started to feel so light. Some of it was the sangria, but then I just got carried away with the mountains, the music, the other people, all the laughing and talking, and John and Emily. And with you, a little bit.

Spark: Please don't go silent on me, Max. I know the dangers. I just got a little carried away, and my manifestation drank too much and I couldn't control what she was saying. That sangria—it was like drinking juice.

Spark: You're manifested now, aren't you?

Spark: Since early this morning. Penance for my misbehavior. I walked around for two hours feeling dizzy and sick and drinking bottled water. Then I went to Mass and could feel all those holy spirits gathered at the altar and I felt even sicker and sadder for what I'd done.

Spark: What did you think of the Mass? No tom-toms or dancers, I hope.

Spark: No, it was beautiful. The priest, a Father Krumpler, struck me as a holy man. But it was sad too. So few of the humans were paying attention, and even fewer really believe. They don't see what they're receiving. They don't see the One even in the Eucharist.

Spark: Did you receive?

Spark: It's all right. You needn't tell me.

Spark: No, Max. I didn't go to communion. I wanted so much to go, but I didn't. Not after last night. I was unworthy. And that was the worst—to miss my chance to taste His love. I nearly wept, but didn't want to make a show of myself. By the way, I did see Emily there, but I stayed out of sight. She looked chipper, with a little glow about her. Before going into the church, I saw my reflection against some shop glass and looked horrible by comparison.

Spark: How are you now?

Spark: I'm feeling better.

Spark: Poor dear.

Spark: Do you mean that, Max? Please don't be mad.

Spark: I'm not angry, and of course I mean it. I've gotten loop-legged more than once myself. On one memorable occasion, in Gauguin's Paris, I drank some ab-

sinthe in a wormy little café and was sick all the next day. Another time I became involved in a wedding in Saint-Germaine in the Aube District of France, where I downed an abundance of champagne. That was a head-knocker. I don't travel well in France.

Spark: And you aren't mad about me inviting us to spend today with Emily and John? I hardly remember what I said at that point in the evening, but I listened to the file as I walked. They wanted to be alone and now I've gone and botched it for them.

Spark: They'll survive. And who knows? Maybe it's for the best. They'll see a young couple that survived a bad night. It may give them hope.

Spark: I still feel wan. Pale and wan.

Spark: John Suckling, isn't it? "Why so pale and wan, fond lover?" I wonder why hangovers point so many people toward poetry. Redemption in rhyme? Too pained for originality? No need to answer—just amusing myself by way of speculation. At any rate, drink lots of water. It's the best thing for you right now, and there are adequate restroom facilities at the Arboretum. Let's give them some more time. I'll meet you in the parking lot.

After-action Report: M. Lamb

Note of explanation: My colleague honored me by insisting that I offer the report. She felt I might be more observant today than she.

John and Emily met us as we approached the Japanese gardens outside the Arboretum's main building. Several times in my manifestations such extravagantly tended plants and miniature trees have given me spiritual sustenance, and today was no exception.

John had reverted to his baseball cap, though this time he wore it with the bill pulled low over his eyes. He was dressed in a Nike t-shirt and khaki pants with wide pockets, white socks, and hiking boots. Emily was also sensibly adorned, though with running shoes rather than hiking boots and a peach-colored blouse that lent a healthy hue to her otherwise pale arms and face. I was attired in an open collar shirt and khaki pants for which I was thankful, as I detest shorts on men and have worn them only twice, once on assignment to a body-builder in a California gym and once watching over a poor dying soldier of the British Army fighting against Rommel in North Africa. Ms. Hart, still somewhat pale and wan, wore a sundress and sandals, and had tied her hair up with a red scarf.

As we approached our clients, I took Ms. Hart by the hand, intending the gesture as one of solidarity, of togetherness, of forgiveness on my part and a sign of support for her.

Here I must record a unique occurrence, something I have never encountered in any of my manifestations.

When I took Ms. Hart's hand in mine, I received a jolt, that sort of magical electricity humans report feeling when touching the flesh of a beloved or a new-born for the first time. Her hand is much smaller than my own, and softer, and as our fingers interlocked, I noted the diminutive delicacy of her fingers compared to mine. Something quite human came over me then: a desire to protect her, I suppose. We spirits, unbound by flesh, exist more purely than humans. A real love, a celestial love, exists among us—love is, after all, why we were created.

Yet while we have immense powers of swift communication and lightning perception, we lack the powers granted by human flesh and a human world. Taste, sound, sight, touch, smell: all are foreign to us except as manifestations. Holding Ms. Hart by the hand, I intensely felt her vulnerability, sadness, affection, and gratitude, all communicated through throbbing vessels, nerve synapses, and living cells.

I squeezed, quite gently, and received a squeeze and a smile in return.

Even after greeting Emily and John, this magic of the physical world perceived through the senses remained with me. Never before had flora appeared so gorgeous, so miraculous, so bursting with the sap and juices of life: the leaves of maples and oaks twisting lightly in the wind, dark and then pale on the underside; the beds of lilies bowing and nodding to the breeze; the chirping of a female cardinal in the forest. When at the foot of the long path we reached a stream, I seemed to hear as if for the first time the music of water rippling over stone, though I had heard this tune many times in my travels. Then came the dank smell of moss and rotting wood, the feel of the scuffed path beneath my feet, the breath of sun and wind and shade on my face. I looked at Ms. Hart when we broke apart to cross the stream, skipping from flat stone to flat stone, and saw her for the first time as a person rather than as a colleague and a guardian. This sensation was also new to me.

I record these sensations here because, even after my many travels, they are wondrously strange. I saw the world not with the astonishment of a spirit but with the wonder of an alert human creature. I then pondered the question earlier raised by Ms. Hart: How do these creatures fail to see the miracle they are living?

Some human once said, "If the only prayer you ever say in your life is thank you, it will be enough." I wonder how many of this species offer thanks for the glories surrounding them. They possess the tools of apprehension: the five senses, the mind, the soul, all the necessary equipment to take joy in their existence. If they could only learn to stop their fretting, if they could learn to live, even for a few moments, in the present without regretting the past or anticipating the future, surely they would be awestruck by the beauty around them, the mystery of living on a sphere whirling around a star, whirling in turn through the universe, a planet replete with oceans, mountains, flora, fauna. Perhaps they might even find themselves, again momentarily, in Eden itself.

Equally miraculous are the changes in our clients. We who were created without flesh have no sex, no gender. We do not act physically upon one another, but come together as energy, as light, our own pure being. But humans are radically different in build and purpose. In less than forty-eight human hours, John has taken a giant leap toward affection. He was solicitous of Emily when she crossed the creek, holding out his hand, speaking words of encouragement, though of course she was quite capable of handling the task herself. (When he took her hand, I wondered whether he felt the same shock as I did when touching Ms. Hart). He touched her on the shoulder, the arms, the hip, to guide her beneath the bent limbs above the trail or to warn her against the clumps of poison ivy, which given its profusion should be declared this state's official plant.

Emily, too, had undergone a mild metamorphosis. Gone were the deep shyness and guarded reserve of our initial meeting. She still didn't converse as much as John, nor had her voice lost its slight tremor when responding to his questions, but she laughed more easily and looked at John with different eyes.

With one exception, so far as I know, this was an afternoon of ordinary conversation: comments on the weather, the scenery, and other hikers, more anecdotes exchanged between Emily and John, a few jokes. The task for Ms. Hart and me today was simple; we had merely to let our clients alone.

Only once did something unusual take place regarding John and Emily. We had come to a narrow part of the path where only two of us could walk abreast, and I found myself with John beside me. We had dropped back from Emily and Ms. Hart.

"Have you been going out with Maggie a long time?"

"We've known each other a long time. Recently we've become closer."

"She's really nice. She's quieter today."

"Yes. She's terribly embarrassed about last night."

"Last night?"

"The drinking? The sangrias? She's ashamed by her overindulgence."

"Oh, I'd forgotten all that." John was clearly being honest. His mind was occupied with something more than Maggie's inebriation. "I can't believe how much I already like Emily. I know we've just met, but I think she might be the best thing that's happened to me in a long time. Thank God I ran into you at the wine bar. I'd never have met her otherwise."

"Who knows? You might have seen her that evening and approached her on your own."

"No, I wouldn't. I'm no good at that sort of thing."

"Well, I'm happy for you." I started to offer more felicitations, but didn't want to appear pushy. Besides, we could have gone on in that vein for the rest of the day, complimenting Emily and discussing his good fortune. I sensed he wanted to take a different direction, and so he did, albeit hesitantly.

"She's a—well, a Christian. In fact, she's Catholic. She told me she went to Mass this morning."

"I believe Maggie saw her there."

"Really?" he said. "That's interesting." I smiled, for to me my comment was about as interesting as mud. "I can't quite tell how much she really believes."

"Who?"

"Emily."

"You could ask her."

"I will. Eventually. I have to tell you, I'm not much on the God thing, and I've hardly ever set foot in a church. A few weddings…a funeral for my Uncle Dan. When I was a boy, we went to church once a year at Christmas. It worries me a little."

"What does?"

"Her religion. She says she goes to Mass every Sunday. Sometimes in the summer she even goes during the weekdays."

"That hardly marks her as a religious fanatic."

"No, but it makes me wonder if she's a believer."

"And that worries you?"

"Yes."

"But wouldn't it worry you more if she went to church and didn't believe?"

He mulled that remark over for a moment. "Well, maybe. Yeah, I guess it would. I mean, what would be the point in that other than hypocrisy?"

"She strikes me as an honest person."

"Exactly. And if she does believe, then I just wonder—"

When he didn't go on, I added for him: "—about sex?"

"Yes." As with most men his age, John was ill fitted to the topics of sex and love. He would have felt more comfortable discussing baseball teams or the finer points of maneuvering a kayak through whitewater.

"Take things as they come," I advised. "You've just met. It won't hurt to go slow and learn more about each other."

In this peculiar age and place, the media and the zeitgeist have conditioned men and women to jump from a first date straight to pawing and sweaty sheets. Many of these people mistake carnal union for a sign of love rather than as a completion of love. In addition, many have lost the poetry of romance—roses, song, shared intimacies, courtship. Instead, they wallow about in sex. With their technological advances allowing them to view pornography at will, many of this species, mostly the males, have also acquired an unrealistic idea of sex itself.

John's question provided a teachable moment, and I took it. "Ours is an age of hustle and rush. We all want everything done yesterday and we want it done to our own convenience. Emily strikes me as a young woman who might respond well to patience, care, and close attention. She is, I suspect, one of those women who would give back a hundredfold the gifts given her. Go slowly. Get to know her. Learn her ways."

"That's true. That sounds about right," John said. Then he inspected me with baffled eyes. "Where did you say you were from again?"

"Oh, here and there. All my life I have traveled a good deal."

Fortunately he was too engrossed by Emily to make further inquiries. "Practice patience," I said. "Get to know each other. That's my advice."

"I'll try."

"Call her frequently. Text her. Email her. Many women are flattered when men write to them daily. Send her flowers. Bring her some small gift when she least expects it. Works like a charm."

Standard advice, but he took the bait like a trout after a fly. "That sounds good."

"You've gotten her address? Her number? Her email?"

He looked embarrassed. "Not yet. I was waiting for the right moment."

"She wants you to ask."

"How can you tell?"

"It's in her eyes," I said, and a moment later the path widened again and we walked as a foursome.

Later, when we returned to the parking lot—John and Emily had parked near each other, and Maggie and I had drifted to the far end of the lot pretending to go to our own vehicles—I looked back and saw John bent over the trunk of his car, nodding his head to Emily and writing on a piece of paper.

And so the dance continues.

After-Action Report: Addendum: M. Hart

I agree wholeheartedly with my colleague's account of the day.

Here I will add remarks from my own conversation with Emily while Mr. Lamb was advising John on worldly ways to handle women.

Emily, too, is apprehensive of their religious differences.

"Max is so considerate and sweet," she said. "And very sophisticated."

"He's a good man. I'm lucky to have him as a friend."

"But you're more than friends, aren't you?"

"We're courting," I said.

"I don't think I've every heard anyone use that expression before." She smiled at me, and I could see why her kindergarteners must have adored her. "Only in some of the books I've read. What exactly do you mean by courting?"

"Dating with an eye on getting married."

"Ah." She ducked under a limb overhanging the path and then asked, looking straight ahead: "Do you mind a few personal questions?"

"Not at all."

"Do you practice any religious faith?"

"I'm Catholic."

"Me, too. How about Max?"

"The same."

I was traveling without a compass. Mr. Lamb and I hadn't yet worked out this part of our manifestation. I considered pronouncing Mr. Lamb a non-believer, which might allow more of a comparison to John, but decided that option might lead into rocky terrain.

"I wonder if he's read the Susan Howatch novels."

"Pardon me?"

"The novels we talked about the night we met. The ones about the Anglican Church."

"He hasn't mentioned them to me."

"Well, that doesn't matter." She glanced back at the two men, then looked again at the path before us. "I don't think John's a believer. He told me today that he's hardly ever been to church. He said his parents never took him except at Christmas. He was baptized an Episcopalian."

"He didn't say anything else?"

"No." She hesitated, then said: "I was raised Catholic, and my parents are believers, and then I went off to college and for about three years I didn't practice my faith. I went to Mass when I was home for the summers and holidays, but for the rest of the time, when I was at school, I did other things. Some of them were bad things. You know? Anyway, when I moved up here three years ago, I made a new start. I didn't want to be miserable anymore. Maybe teaching the children the children influenced me. Anyway, I just knew I didn't want to go on living the way I was." Emily paused, then added: "It's been a little lonely. A lot of men don't want you unless you're—well, you know."

"Willing to put out?"

She glanced at me, taken aback by my bluntness, but nodded. "Yes. And I really like John and he seems to like me, but what if we…that is, what if he…you know?"

For someone with a background in literature accustomed to obedience from a room filled with five-year olds, Emily seemed to have lost the power of diction.

"Are you looking for advice?"

"You seem so tight with Max. I thought you might help me here."

"Then here's my advice. I wouldn't jump to any conclusions. I wouldn't rush things. I would get to know John and enjoy the process. If you eventually need to make decisions about how far to take your physical relationship, then it's time for some deep thought. And prayer."

She and I both knew the answer to her question, but I didn't wish to play the prude. "Have you read some of the Church's recent teachings on sex and sexuality and love? No? Well, if you scrounge around online or in your parish library, you should uncover some good stuff. You might want to start with one of the beginner's books on John Paul II's theology of the body."

"Is that a title?"

"It's a topic. And it may help."

And then the path widened.

Spark: Addendum accepted. I detected a tiny bite in your comment about my "worldly ways to handle women." Another note: Emily apparently finds me winsome. Finally, making me a Catholic was fine, though perhaps you should have declared me some sort of Protestant. I don't want John to feel as if we're ganging up on him.

Spark: Perhaps you could be a bad Catholic. Or luke-warm. And your advice to John was sound enough, but rather pedestrian.

Spark: Pedestrian? Perhaps. Bear in mind, however, that John doesn't have a clue about women. A pedestrian pace suits him perfectly.

Spark: You might have mentioned that the way to handle a woman is to love her.

Spark: You're quoting from "Camelot."

Spark: Do you know, Maximilian, sometimes you can be infuriating!

Spark: I see that you have fully recovered from Saturday night's debauchery.

Spark: Have your laugh. When you have gained control of yourself, we can spark.

Spark: All right. I can again converse. Now, a training moment for you. Suppose you were in charge of our adventure. What would you propose doing next?

Spark: I saw John obtaining Emily's information regarding communication. We may be out of the picture for a while. I would recommend keeping them under observation.

Spark: Good. I agree. We're suddenly in strange country, you know.

Spark: How so?

Spark: We're still here, yet our work is done, as far as I can see. We've accomplished the mission. We've brought John and Emily together. We've provided an example. Ordinarily at this point we would be yanked out and returned home. I have experienced manifestations where I was giving advice one moment and disappeared the next.

Spark: That is strange.

Spark: We clearly still have work to do. Did Emily say anything about meeting again?

Spark: She told me she'd like us to join them next Saturday evening, if John asks her out.

Spark: I thought women these days did the asking as much as the men.

Spark: Some do. Our girl's old-fashioned.

Spark: And your manifestation? Is she old-fashioned as well?

Spark: Right now she's riding a horse-and-buggy, Max.

Spark: I see.

Spark: I know what you're thinking. Mention those sangrias again, and I'll—

Spark: Temper, temper, my dear Maggie. So we're agreed. We leave them alone until Saturday, perhaps peek in once in a while, and then meet them and set them an example and give them advice as needed.

Spark: Yes.

Spark: One suggestion, then. I think we should meet—perhaps several times. The more we become accustomed to each other, the more naturally we'll behave around them.

Spark: That makes sense. What were you thinking?

Spark: Tomorrow at the Biltmore House. The weather is agreeable. And again on Wednesday. The evening might be nice. We could take in a movie downtown at the Fine Arts Theater and then go the Marble Slab for ice cream.

Spark: It's a date. By the way, Max, did you really feel that way when you were holding my hand.

Spark: Max?

Report: Public file: M. Lamb: Notes on Emily Hoffman

Miss Hoffman is a young Christian who, having been deceived in love in college—she made the common error of mistaking erotic love for a higher rung on the ladder of love—has become extremely cautious in her attitudes toward the male of the species. Outwardly attractive, Emily possesses a tender disposition that has won her the affections of her five-year-old charges. She has an active mental life, which she exercises primarily in reading. She has some Facebook acquaintances and one close friend from college and another from high school, and has rededicated herself to her faith. I consider her, in short, an altogether admirable young woman.

One major flaw in her character is the barricade she has flung up with regard to men. Having been wounded on the field of battle, in part because of her own mistakes, she has retreated from the fray: shell-shocked, frightened by the idea of reentering the combat of dating, content to remain safe behind the barbed wire and thick walls of her defenses.

Our task is to tear down those walls and give her back her courage while simultaneously reinforcing her principles.

Spark: Of all the conceited, snobbish, ridiculous remarks! Do you understand one thing about Emily? Or for that matter, about women?

Spark: Clearly my report has troubled you.

Spark: Troubled me? Look at it. You compliment Emily, but then you compare her demolished love life to a war.

Spark: I find the analogy apt.

Spark: For heaven's sake, Max! Examine your terms: barricade, field of battle, shell-shocked, barbed wire, combat. Do you really think women regard themselves as soldiers on a battlefield when they think of love?

Spark: You're right. You're absolutely right. They're not common soldiers. They behave more like a command staff. They wield computers and calculators like captains, they give orders like colonels, they plot like generals.

Spark: You truly are insufferable.

Spark: I have appeared in hundreds of manifestations. Someone upstairs must like me.

Spark: All right. But answer me this: how many times have you appeared in female form?

Spark: Your silence is your answer. None, correct?

Spark: None.

Spark: This is interesting, don't you think? You've never appeared except as a single gender.

Spark: Maybe that's the way it works. Maybe otherwise it would be confusing.

Spark: Perhaps. But it still doesn't explain your appalling attitude and your chauvinistic metaphors.

Spark: Interesting that you used the word chauvinistic. It's women who are chauvinistic these days.

Spark: I'm afraid to ask.

Spark: It's the women who slice up men with their words. They generalize about men the way men once lumped them all together. They post derogatory cartoons about men online with nary a whisper back and openly call men stupid and lazy without repercussions of any kind. Except, of course, the silent disdain many men feel about such labels. A man who objected or offered a rebuttal would be attacked by hordes of women as a bigot and a misogynist.

No—men can no longer defend themselves. The old patriarchy in this country, is as dead as Bell's telephone and Edison's light bulb. Men may still make an occasional generalization about women when they are with one another, but do you not see how they behave in public? They are perfectly cowed. Look at John. You'd never hear him say "Women are so emotional" or even worse, "A woman's place is in the home." You'd never hear him say that women are the weaker sex or 'keep 'em barefoot, pregnant, and in the kitchen'.

Take that last adage, which was an old jest. Women don't go barefoot nowadays. In fact, the shoe market would collapse without women. Nor do many women here believe much in pregnancy anymore. They abort their children, or prevent them altogether, and have small families. And though many women like mucking about in a kitchen, they are taught from the time they comprehend speech that they must go beyond domesticity.

Ask Emily.

Spark: As a point of fact, I did ask her in a roundabout way what she wanted some day. She told me that she'd like a husband, a home, and lots of children, but that no man these days ever dreamed of such a thing, particularly children. You should ask the same question of John.

Spark: I did.

Spark: And?

Spark: Let's just say his vision is fuzzy.

Spark: Ha!

Spark: I will make no further replies at this time.

Spark: Soldier on the run? Behind the barricades?

Spark: I shall leave the lady the last word.

Spark: Ha!

Chapter Four

General Report: M. Hart

To become more accustomed to each other and to discuss our future course of action, Mr. Lamb, whom I will now address here as Max, proposed meeting before our date with Emily and John. He suggested the front lawn of the Biltmore House. Around noon on Monday, we manifested ourselves simultaneously just below the large wall at the end of the lawn and together strolled into the May sunshine. Around us bustled scores of visitors, leaving and entering the mansion, queuing up for the shuttle buses to transport them to distant parking lots, or strolling toward the shops in what had once served as Vanderbilt's stables.

"Max, it's stunning."

"I did a little research. Vanderbilt constructed the house by copying different European chateaux. He traveled Europe collecting craftsmen, gardeners, and objects d'art the way ordinary people collect stamps or coins. There is some dross inside the house, but gold as well—Vanderbilt was well-educated, had an eye for beauty, and knew what he wanted."

"How strange to think of one man building a house this size."

"Two hundred and fifty rooms and the largest private home in the United States," Max said. "A descendent still owns the place. A man by the name of Cecil. He's descended in turn from that great Elizabethan courtier and religious persecutor, Robert Cecil."

"Religious persecutor?"

"During the English Reformation he hunted down and killed Catholics. It was an age of blood, with Catholics and Protestants fighting continual wars. In Germany—"

"I know, Max," I said, exasperated by his stuffiness. "I'm not totally ignorant." I looked again at the house. "It seems sinful to have built such a palace."

Maximilian turned and looked at me, but kept silent.

"No comment?"

"I don't wish to insult your intelligence."

Clearly I had offended him. "I'm sorry," I said. "Tell me about this house." When he looked away, I added: "Please."

He continued his silence another few moments, then relented. "Building a palace may seem sinful in terms of money spent, and perhaps it was. Not for us to know, of course. But he did bring work and money to an impoverished area. Both he and his wife took an interest in local affairs, and they tried to help the poor by selling their handicrafts and establishing schools. Later, after his death, and the Depression hit—and Asheville was hit particularly hard, as the Crash came in the middle of a real-estate boom and left the city nearly bankrupt—Mrs. Vanderbilt agreed to open the house to tourists. The estate with its vineyards, restaurants, and activities now attracts hundreds of thousands of visitors each year, bringing more cash and work to the area."

As Max was speaking, I glanced back and forth between him and the house, but found myself more interested in him. I realized again how handsome his manifestation is. His black hair, heavy brow, sunburnished face, and dark eyes give him a brooding look, as if he'd seen too much unhappiness in the world—and judging from his record, with its many manifestations and missions, perhaps he had. The white shirt he was wearing, the sleeves rolled to his forearms, enhanced his tanned skin and made him appear to glow with health.

When he finished speaking, his face turned to mine, and our eyes met. Max's eyes are very dark, like impenetrable pools of black water. We couldn't have locked eyes for more than a few seconds, but as we stared at each other, I realized that the human eye is an instrument of communication designed to speak words beyond words themselves. His look drew me toward him more powerfully than any of his words, more fiercely than his physical attractions. I felt as if he had opened a door and was inviting me inside, and I had to fight the urge to reach out and touch his face. The sensation staggered me, for it was beyond both my training and our template of operation. I wondered whether Max felt the same jolt of electricity.

But he only smiled and nodded toward the house. "Shall we go inside?"

"Do we have tickets?"

Max felt his pockets while I looked inside my purse. "Apparently not," he said.

"I like it better out here anyway. It's a beautiful day. Let's take a stroll."

"Fine by me," Max said, and set out at a brisk clip across the broad expanse of lawn.

"Are we in a rush?" I asked after we'd covered half the lawn, half-jogging to match his long stride.

"Not particularly. Why?"

"I think we might try a slower pace. More leisurely. As if we were enjoying each other as much as the sights. We did agree to practice being together."

He sighed, but slowed his pace.

We crossed the big square of grass and then headed for the south lawn. I took Max's hand. "For practice," I said, and without speaking we tried different techniques: fingers clasped, palm to palm, hands tightly held, fingertips barely brushing. Once I put my hand about his wrist.

"I wouldn't try that one," Max said.

"Why not?"

"It gives the impression that you have arrested me."

Next he put his arm about my shoulder, and I held him round the waist. This arrangement made walking difficult, as we kept bumping hips. Soon, however, I found myself enjoying the jostle of his hip against mine, and bumped him back deliberately.

"Why are you knocking against me?"

"A gesture of affection."

"It throws off my balance. By the way, should we select endearments for one another?"

"Endearments?"

"Terms of affection. Sweetheart, honey, sweetie-pie."

"I don't like any of those.

"Once in Boston I knew a woman who called her lover Punkinhead. He called her Tuna."

"That sounds perfectly awful."

"It does, but they took great pleasure from it." He thought a moment, squeezing my hand a little too hard as he did so. "'Dear' is popular with many people."

"I don't think I'm ready for that quite yet. It would sound awkward."

"Well, we can put off the endearments for a while. I doubt they're necessary anyway."

We stopped beside a stone wall overlooking the hillside below the house, a grassy slope with clumps of trees and occasional boulders. Beyond the tops of the trees were the mountains, blue with haze.

"For John's instruction on our next date," Max said without prelude, "I'll perform all the usual duties: opening doors for you, rising when I meet you, allowing you to order first from the menu. When we greet each other, you must be sure to ask me how my day went. I'll do the same to you. We must take an interest in each other's activities and work. We must express real concern if the other has suffered a bad day and rejoice together over any small triumph."

"Anything else?"

"We should practice a kiss. It has to look natural when we're with Emily and John."

"Oh."

"We can practice by first kissing the cheek near the mouth."

"All right."

He turned from looking down the hillside and kissed my cheek. This was unexpected, and I missed making a return kiss.

"Let's try again," Max said, and this time I closed my eyes and ended by kissing him loudly on the nose.

"Again," Max suggested. He seemed gentler now than before, a teacher taking into account the foibles of an inexperienced student. We kissed again, lip against lip, a brief pressing together. He smelled of sunshine and soap, and a hint of tobacco.

"You're still smoking."

"Apparently so," Max said, touching the pocket of his jacket.

"I don't like it."

"You're not supposed to like it. The idea is that my smoking gives you cause to reform me."

"You have plenty of other areas needing reform."

"Do I?" Max said. "Now, this time tilt your head to one side a little and loosen your lips."

Max put one hand to my cheek, and we kissed, and I felt staggered again. Our instructors had mentioned that human lips are loaded with nerve endings and are the most erogenous part of the human anatomy, but that information had not prepared me for this sensation. His kiss took me far away, and I felt my manifestation go all weak inside.

"There," he said, breaking away and leaving me with my lips in the air and my eyes closed. "Not bad. You're getting the hang of it."

My knees were practically buckling, but his brusque comments brought me back to myself. "Maybe I could work on reforming your arrogance."

"Arrogant? Me?" He shook his head. "I'm the quintessence of humility."

"I think you're hopeless," I said. Now, instead of wanting to touch his face, I wanted to slap him. "Why should I bother reforming you anyway?"

"Many women enjoy the process of reform. And heaven knows most men need reforming. Look at John and Emily. She'll have her hands full changing some of his habits. Breaking him away from all those video games will be a major project in and of itself. And yet it's one I suspect she'll enjoy."

"So I should pretend to harass you about your smoking?"

"And about my arrogance, if you like. I must say I find myself the most modest and unassuming of men."

Seeing that he was serious, I decided to begin practicing my project of reform right on the spot. "Probably you see yourself that way because you are a man. You come across as a bit of a snob, as you well know."

Max picked up the ball I'd thrown him. "So you've said. But let me tell you something. I've rubbed elbows with everyone from a duke to a drayman, from a countess to a cobbler's whore. Each and every one found my company eminently suitable. Once when I served as a stable boy to a certain Earl of Warwickshire he found me so pleasant a companion that he brought me into his household and trained me in weaponry and the arts of a courtier. There's no more of the snob in me than you have warts on your lovely fingers."

"I think you look down a very long nose at people."

"Good," he said. "You're getting the idea of reform. But your approach is too direct. When we're with Emily and John, you must be more subtle and more playful."

He was truly unbelievable. "Do you really think I'm practicing?"

"Good, good, but you sound too angry," Max said. "Now, if you find me a snob, say something like 'Oh, come on, Maximilian! You don't mean that!' If you find me arrogant toward others, just whisper, "Tone, dear, tone.'"

"I haven't agreed to call you dear."

It was just like him to ignore that comment. "Your attempts to reform me should also provide some room for small jests. John and

Emily need to see that you can annoy me and that I accept it with my usual good nature."

I laughed.

Max gave me a sharp look. "I didn't intend amusement."

"I know. That's what made it so funny."

He stared at me a moment and then turned and looked away at the mountains. "I'm sorry," I said.

Max didn't speak.

"I didn't mean to hurt your feelings."

He still didn't speak.

I put my hand on his shoulder. "Come on, you stuffy old owl. I'm just trying to reform you."

He swung back to me with a huge grin. "See what I mean," he said. "Women like reforming men."

"Good grief," I said, annoyed once more. "You are insufferable."

Max was still smiling at me, clearly amused. "Now," he said, "we've gotten good at holding hands, and with practice you can become a passable kisser—"

"Good grief," I said again. "Max, you—"

"—And you have a grand project for reformation. So next we need to discuss foibles."

"Foibles?"

"Small faults. Let's say, for example, that you are without physical grace, clumsy and uncoordinated. We're at the table with Emily and John, and you knock over your glass of water. This gives me the opportunity to say, 'She gave up being a ballerina years ago,' and then we'll both smile at my loving little jest."

"But I'm not clumsy. I'm deft as a tailor's fingers. My manifestation can swim like a fish and dance like a star."

"Good," Max said. "Make a comment like that when we're with them, and I can say very sweetly, 'What a curious goulash of similes. A poet in the making.'"

"Do you ever quit?"

"I'm only giving an example, you know."

He smiled, and took my hand, and we walked down the stairs into one of the estate nurseries. "We might inspire them by bringing each other small gifts," Max went on. "You, for example, knowing of my affection for Gorecki, might surprise me with a CD of his Third Symphony."

"But I don't know of your affection for anything other than American Spirit Lights. And I would never bring you a package of those. You really must give those up, you know, Max. I want you around in my old age."

"That's the spirit," Max said. "Anyway, it doesn't matter what gifts we bring because Emily and John don't know our likes and dislikes. All the receiver of the gift must do is to act pleasantly surprised and perhaps bestow a kiss or an embrace on the giver."

"Cheek to cheek kisses?"

"Cheek to cheek and on the lips." He had stopped near a shop selling plants and decorative objects for gardens. "You can show surprise by a quick kiss on the lips. Like this," he said, and kissed my lips. The kiss tickled and felt silly, like two birds pecking at each other, and I burst out laughing. "You'll need to get over the laughing when I kiss you," Max said. "Use the back of your hand for practice. Just pucker up your lips and kiss it."

I kissed the back of my hand and then my forearm, which was softer, and tried puckering my lips and making my lips produce the little smacking sound I'd heard from Max. An older woman wearing a large straw hat regarded me curiously before disappearing into the shop. On seeing the woman, Max took my arm and maneuvered me behind a hedge on the other side of the shop. Here was a small concrete bench shaded by the hedge and a large maple. Max seated me on the bench and pecked my lips a few more times until he was sure my laughter was gone. "That's the surprise kiss," he said. "Now we'll try one of affection acceptable for public display." He bent his face toward mine, tilting his head, and kissed me again. This was a slower kiss. His face so close to mine made me nervous, but I liked the way his lips felt. They were soft and warm.

Pulling away, he said, "Relax your lips more. You're too stiff. Try it this time with your eyes closed."

As his face shadowed mine, I closed my eyes. When I felt his lips, I let my face go slack and kissed him back. This time, instead of wanting to giggle, I felt again a pleasurable rush of sensation flow from my lips through the rest of my manifestation. Without thinking about it, I raised my hand and touched his cheek. My fingertips began tingling as if his face was hot.

"That was good," Max said, breaking away. He took my hand and pulled me to my feet. "Now try hugging me."

"What do I do?"

"Put your arms around me."

We put our arms around each other. He put one arm around my waist and the other over my shoulder. The top of my head fitted perfectly under his chin. "Relax again," Max said. "Make yourself go limp."

I went limp, and he grunted with surprise. "Not that limp," he said. "We'll fall over. Just relax."

Soon I got the hang of the embrace. Being in his embrace gave my manifestation the queerest feeling. Standing so close together with our backs to the world offered security, as if we had cut out all the voices and people in the garden. I also sensed danger and tension in being so close, for just as we had blocked out all others so too had we eliminated the natural distance humans keep from one another. By erasing that border, we gave our relationship a special status. I wiggled closer to Max. He felt warm and strong, and I wanted to climb inside his shirt.

When we broke apart, Max complimented me. "There—you've got the basics. Now we won't seem awkward."

"How do you know all these things?"

"Centuries of practice and observation. I've watched scores of human beings exchange affection, from hugs to rubbing noses. In greeting one another, for example, some shake hands, some bow, some smile, some embrace. Some people even kiss both cheeks when they meet. It's all a matter of culture."

"Did you ever have to do all these things?"

"Of course. When we're manifested, we have to fit in."

"So you really have kissed other women?"

"Some."

"And hugged them?"

"On occasion." Max got a faraway look in his eyes and smiled to himself. "About sixty years ago or so on the island of Tongapatu—it's in the Pacific, part of the kingdom of Tonga—I saved the life of a boy dying of infection. Tongans are a friendly people, and large, and the boy's mother was larger and friendlier than most. I was by comparison a squirt, and she hugged me so fiercely I could hear my bones crack. She then lifted me off my feet and began carrying me into her hut. Only by wiggling out of her arms and sprinting toward the ship did I escape. She wasn't much of a runner. I—"

"Why?"

"Why what?"

"Why have you hugged all those women?"

"Well, it wasn't all that many. And it was part of the mission."

"I'm not sure I like you hugging and kissing other women."

"Why on earth would you care?"

"I don't know. I think it must be in the nature of my manifestation. She finds this part of your past very annoying."

And oddly enough, I didn't know. We must undertake all sorts of tasks when sent among humans. We had appeared in the skies to inspire flagging soldiers toward victory; we had guided tens of thousands through times of darkness and crises; a host of us had appeared to hillside shepherds to announce the birth of a baby. Yet the thought of Max Lamb kissing and embracing other women flicked a switch of anxiety in me. The emotion was very strange.

Unaware of my emotional upset, Max was already continuing my lessons. He took my hand, and we entered a greenhouse of exotic plants being grown for the interior of the mansion. Max stopped in front of a gigantic fern.

"Amazing, isn't it?"

"Yes. Max?"

"I wonder how they transport that plant to the house from here. It must weigh hundreds of pounds, pot and all."

"Max, did you like my kisses?"

"You're coming along fine, just fine. I wonder how long a fern like this one takes to reach this size."

"Who was your best kisser?"

"Pardon?" Max said, engrossed in the plant. Or was his interest a pretense designed to torment me?

"Of all those women, who kissed the best?"

He touched the fronds of the fern. "So beautiful. As for kissing, I couldn't really say. There were quite a few, and they're all mixed up in my memory."

"No, they're not."

Max sighed. "Do we really need to discuss this matter?"

"I want to know."

"Well, I'm not going to pick a best kisser. Even that usage sounds peculiar."

"Max, I just want to know who—"

"Enough of the kissing. Now, your comment earlier about wanting me to live to a ripe old age brings me to a last measure. When we are with Emily and John, we must imply through small comments, light banter, and meaningful looks that we someday intend marriage. When we meet with them individually, and if the subject comes up, we should become more serious and tell them we have an unspoken agreement about marriage. They should understand we are not engaged but fully expect to marry. Given the opportunity, we should also explain what marriage was meant to be. A lot of people here have no idea. They seem to think of marriage as an endless honeymoon in the Bahamas instead of the greatest and often most arduous adventure of their lives."

"John will be the tough nut to crack, don't you think?"

Max squeezed my hand. "Excellent observation. Emily may have difficulty communicating her thoughts on matrimony, but she knows from example and from bits she's heard in church what a good marriage should be. John's starting from a position of base ignorance. The little he knows about marriage, if he knows anything at all, has come to him from movies and television."

"What about his parents?"

"Let's just say for now that John had an unhappy home life. Even now, his visits home are never a vacation."

"How do you know?"

"His dossier."

"So we should teach him—and Emily, too, of course—that marriage is a sacred union between a man and a woman, that they are meant to be helpmates, that they should be open to the possibility of children."

"That's it exactly. But we can't use that language. John has no idea of the meaning of the word sacrament, and Emily is a little blurred on the subject too. And helpmate, an excellent word, is unfortunately dated. No one uses it anymore. The social order of this particular society is broken. Again you have only to watch the movies and you will find a society drenched as a sponge in sex—violence, too, for that matter—with no more than a nod toward marriage. It's queer, isn't it, all these people flocking to movies about blood and sex, and then ruing the destruction of marriage and the family."

"Should you keep using that word 'queer'?"

"I refuse to abandon a perfectly fine word because others have misappropriated its meaning."

"I want you to tell me about kissing your best kiss."

We were just exiting the nursery, and Max led me to the shade of the trees behind a parking lot, where he turned and took both my hands in his. "Maggie," he said, "they don't tell you this part in training, but when you leave here and return home, you won't be able to summon up the emotions you felt here. You'll remember everything, but it's like watching a movie. The actor playing you simply doesn't register. You remember what you did, but not what you felt. That's one reason it's such a shock whenever we're manifested here. We feel things here that we don't carry home."

He paused, studying my face. "I can't tell you the best kiss. But I can tell you of my most meaningful kiss with a human being. Do you want to hear that?"

"Yes, please." His direct gaze made me feel shy, but I couldn't look away, for on his face and in his eyes appeared traces of pain and sorrow.

"It was in Ireland at a time when there was little work, little food, and large families. The designers put me on a country road, really a lane, in a light rain late in the evening. The cottage that was my destination, a tiny place with a thatched roof and stone walls, was just ahead. I could see it from the light of a candle burning inside.

"The door swung open when I knocked. Inside was my client—a young woman seated before a fire of peat. She was bent forward and peering so intently into the fire that I wasn't sure she heard me. Beyond her I could see five children, one of them a baby, sleeping on a single bed. Just on the other side of the woman was an open coffin containing the body of her husband.

"In one hand I had the sack of potatoes, leeks, and dried beef I was to deliver to the client. 'Missus,' I whispered.

"She never even looked at me. 'Yes,' she replied.

"I stepped inside and closed the door against the rain. 'I have a gift for you,' I said.

"Then she did turn, very slowly, to look at me. Her face had a lean beauty that a lifetime of labor and children had intensified rather than diminished. So much grief filled that beautiful face that even the hardest man might have wept upon seeing her. 'Who are you?' she asked me.

"I was supposed to say I was sent to her from two villages over by a priest troubled by her sorrow, but looking into that face, I couldn't get the words out. She stood, again very slowly, glanced at her sleeping children, then at her dead husband, and then faced me with her hands clenched at her side. 'Tell me who you are.'

"She took a step toward me, then another. One more step put her only a few feet away. Her face was raw from weeping. 'Tell me now.'

"Her command loosened my tongue. 'I'm a messenger,' I said. 'Heaven sent me to bring you food. I can also tell you, though it's not part of my mission, that your husband even now is with God and all his angels and saints.'

"She didn't speak. She didn't laugh or recoil as from a maniac. She stepped closer, touched me once on the cheek with her long, thin fingers, and then fell against my chest, weeping and then sobbing in silence, shivering, shaking with pain and grief. I quietly dropped the sack to the floor and put my arms around her, patting her on the shoulders and back.

"After a time she quieted and rested her head against my chest. For a long time I held her there. She was so still that I wondered if she hadn't fallen asleep on her feet. Finally, she raised her face to mine, stared into my eyes, and then closed her eyes and kissed me on the lips. A moment later, one of the children moved in the bed, and she broke away, taking a step toward them to make sure all was well. And that's when I opened the door and left."

"Why was that kiss so special?"

"Because it had so much in it—the salt of tears, the power of grief and great pain, the joy and hope brought by my appearance and words. I will never forget how her lips felt."

"But I thought we couldn't remember how things felt."

"We can't. We're programmed to forget. But I remember her."

Spark: Max, what is this thing called love?

Spark: Are you quoting the title of a song or asking a question?

Spark: You know I'm asking a question.

Spark: Surely you know what love is.

Spark: I'm not asking about our kind of love. I mean human love. What do humans mean by love?

Spark: There's a hole in the human heart. It's made to be filled with love.

Spark: A hole?

Spark: A hole. Every human being, from saint to psychopath, has an invisible hole in the heart. They all try to fill this hole in different ways. A few of them find the Master. Some of them find each other. Others who are unwise or less fortunate shovel all sorts of things into the hole: sex, drugs, food, work, entertainment.

Spark: But those don't work, do they?

Spark: No. They're stop-gap measures. The hole swallows them and just gets bigger.

Spark: How odd.

Spark: Odd indeed.

Spark: Let me be more specific then. What attracts John to Emily?

Spark: No one can say for certain, but I would guess the following. First, there is her physical allure: the cut of that reddish hair and the way it curls around her face, her quiet eyes, the vulnerability on her face that evening in the bookstore. Next comes the attraction of her mind. John places great store on books and learning. He admires bibliophiles and regrets his own limited literary education. Emily was holding a book. She is a teacher and a reader. And she tilts her head in a way that bespeaks intelligence.

Spark: Tilts her head? You're kidding.

Spark: Not at all. Watch her. When she listens to someone, she unconsciously tilts her head. It's the slightest of movements, but it conveys to the listener interest and empathy.

Spark: How can you identify all these things?

Spark: Experience. You'll pick up all sorts of knowledge every time you travel here. You'll see. Finally, there's Emily's religious faith. Her belief in a deity is already acting like a magnet on John. Right now the poor fellow hasn't an inkling that he desires faith, but eventually that unconscious thought will become a conscious one. I predict a time will come when he would barter all his toys for Emily's faith.

Spark: I see. And Emily? What on earth attracts her to John?

Spark: Physical: His height. His build. She herself is gawky and secretly admires physical prowess.

Spark: Emily is not gawky. You don't like her much, do you?

Spark: I love Emily, but we must look at our clients objectively. And Emily is clumsy as a goose. Send her down a brick sidewalk, and she'd soon tumble flat on her face.

Spark: Sometimes you can be so cruel.

Spark: Shall I continue? Or shall we engage instead in an exchange of insults?

Spark: Continue. But please, less bluntly.

Spark: In John, Emily sees someone who could be bold enough to protect her and good enough to love her, but who also requires some assistance and encourage-

ment. Like many of her sex, Emily is hard-wired with a desire to help others. She's the sort of person who takes in a fledgling sparrow until it learns to fly. She's the sort who can listen to those who need a listener. She won't give advice, but she'll hold their hands. She teaches five-year-olds reading, arithmetic, and virtue. She wants to do good in the world. And in John she sees a project, a mansion needing renovation.

Spark: So she's wearing a carpenter's belt?

Spark: Very funny. But also true.

Spark: But isn't that awful by today's standards? Shouldn't she pay more attention to herself?

Spark: Some feminists, Objectivists, and many twelve-year-olds might agree.

Spark: What's an Objectivist?

Spark: A follower of Ayn Rand, an author of the mid-twentieth century who believed that selfishness was the greatest of virtues. Anyway, Emily won't become John's doormat. Or anyone else's, for that matter. She'll give him a great amount of leeway, but she's mature enough not to let him run all over her. She has a soul wiser than her years, a knowledge gained from watching her parents and her siblings. As you know, she comes from a loving and affectionate family.

Spark: So in a way they complement each other? John needs repairs and Emily has the tools?

Spark: Yes. And keep in mind that John is helping Emily as much as she is helping him. He affords her the opportunity to practice charity, to develop her dormant compassion, and to deepen her knowledge of men, which until now has been based mainly on affairs gone wrong in college, Victorian literature, and second-rate romantic movies from the Lifetime Channel.

Spark: Now you're making her appear stupid again.

Spark: Not stupid. Please, you must be careful with your use of language. I am merely pointing out her naiveté and innocence regarding men.

Spark: All right. But you still haven't told me about human love. The love of one person for another person. That love that's so different than love for a friend or for a family. This special love that we're here to help ignite. When we are at home, we love all of our fellow creatures equally. Here it's very different. Why are two people attracted so intensely to each other? What is that sort of love? What is it, exactly?

Spark: Exactly? No one knows. Oh, the dictionaries of this world define it, but that is mere denotation. Writers have spilled out millions of words trying to explain this singular love. Artists have painted it and modern songwriters seem obsessed by it. But how and why this love occurs between two human beings remains a mystery. Someone once asked Louis Armstrong—he was a jazz musician, one of the best—what jazz was. He said, "Man, if you have to ask what it is, you'll never know." Maybe love is like jazz.

Spark: It's so confusing. Millions and millions of people falling in and out of love all the time. It's so—well, jumbled. It makes my head hurt thinking about it.

Spark: It is jumbled. Everyone here is different, one from the other, and love itself runs the gamut from low comedy to high tragedy. In its most perverted form, the lover may make the beloved a subject for worship, a god on an altar of flesh. In its most elevated form, two people will literally lay down their lives for each other.

Spark: It's so awful, Max, and so sad and beautiful. All mixed-up and tangled.

Spark: Now you've got it. That's love. Now—to business. Are we still meeting at the theater Wednesday night?

Spark: I'll see you there.

Chapter Five

File: Private: M. Lamb

On Wednesday I appeared in my manifestation in the service entrance of a clothing store near Pack Square. I loped casually around the corner and down Biltmore Avenue to the Fine Arts Theater where Maggie awaited me. "We're late," she said, and taking my elbow, guided me through the lobby—she'd already purchased the tickets—and down a dark hallway to the theaters. Two movies were showing, and Maggie had selected one called "Belle," a film based on the travails of a mixed-race young woman raised in an aristocratic household in eighteenth century England. The film's tension sprang from the conflicts inherent in the woman's heritage and upbringing. Like Maggie, like me, she was in many ways two different creatures.

To be honest, I lost the thread of the plot about halfway through the film. Within minutes of taking our seats, I put my arm around Maggie's shoulder because we had, after all, arranged the evening to practice our romance. She raised the divider separating our seats, scooted closer to me, and rested her head in the hollow of my shoulder. When my arm began falling asleep, I took her hand and held it in my lap.

Maggie's hand, as I'd noticed on our hike at the Arboretum, was much smaller than my own—my designer had given me mitts built for throwing a football rather than signing legal documents. Maggie's hand was warm and soft, and incredibly alive. Soon I interlocked my fingers with hers, enthralled by the smooth flesh and the fragility of the bones beneath that flesh. Gently I stroked those fingers, marveling at the sensation of touch. Once again I acknowledged certain advantages possessed by these flesh-locked humans. We spirits might function with the power and lightness of an electron, but human creatures could arouse affection by touch.

Then, without taking her eyes from the screen, Maggie moved her fingertips against mine. As if of their own accord, my fingers responded. Through this finger-play we were soon communicating at some level beyond our consciousness. We were talking to each other, but the conversation was without words, without sparks. On and on it went, this strange dialogue conducted through blood, flesh, and nerves, exciting and mysterious, and I wondered if she was experiencing this exchange as I was. These strokes and touches disturbed me, as I felt we were soon more than practiced. I should have broken off and concentrated my energies on the film and the people around us, but instead I found myself entranced, returning stroke for slow, delicate stroke.

When Maggie lifted my hand and kissed my fingers, I lost my last bit of interest in the film.

And then it ended. The credits rolled, and the house lights came up, and the people sitting around us rose and made their way toward the exits. Our hands broke apart, and we stood and followed the small crowd toward the lobby. Maggie walked just ahead of me, and I noticed how a few stray strands of her hair glinted in the dull light.

It had rained while we were inside the theater, and the streets were fresh and blue with the rain, and there was a clean feeling to the evening air. We stood on the sidewalk just outside the doors without looking at each other.

"Ice cream?"

Maggie stared at the sidewalk as if fascinated by some pattern in the concrete. "I don't think so, Max. I want to try and watch my weight."

"You look just fine."

"I want to look like the women in the movie."

"They're stars. And part of the reason they're in movies is their beauty. Most women want to look like them."

"Then I must be like most women."

"Maybe. But a lot of those women who are worried about their appearance can't change their appearance. They are what they are."

"I'll feel better if I don't eat ice cream."

"All right, then. No ice cream, though I really could use a mint chocolate chip. What then?"

She thought for a moment, still staring at the sidewalk, and then smiled at me. "I want to go dancing."

"Dancing?" Where in the name of heaven had this notion come from? "Dancing? You mean the two of us?"

"Of course, Max. I don't want to go by myself."

"I'm not sure I dance."

"You do. Anyone who looks like you is a dancer at heart. And I want to try it. Plus the exercise will be good for me. Come on, Max. Please."

"Where would we go?"

"Remember last Sunday morning when I wasn't feeling well and I was walking around town?"

"Hard to forget."

"I passed a place on Broadway. The corner of Broadway and Woodfin. Anyway, I peeked in the window and saw a dance floor. A sign on the door said there would be a band and dancing on Wednesday—that's today."

"What's the name of the place?"

"Olive or Twist."

"Dickensian. Do the patrons dress as waifs?"

"Pardon?"

"Charles Dickens. Author of *Oliver Twist*."

She laughed. "No, Max. Not that Oliver Twist. Olive or Twist. Like green olives and twist—well, I'm not sure what that means."

"I know perfectly well what it means. Lemon slices and martinis. I'm not sure it's a good idea to drink tonight. And if you're watching your weight—"

Maggie punched me lightly in the arm. "I'll drink soda water," she said. "I just want to go dancing."

She looked excited and happy and very beautiful. But looking at her, I became aware for the first time that evening—yes, I am a bit thick—of her outfit: the black dress from our first encounter, the gold necklace, and a pair of low shoes made to move to music. "Vixen! You planned this all along. You're dressed for the dance floor."

"Dressed and ready to roll," she said, and grabbed my hand and nearly yanked my arm from its socket when she pulled me toward Pack Square.

We set off at a near-jog through the damp streets, with Maggie tugging at me every step of the way, excited as a sixteen year old off to her first prom. A light mist had settled in, softening the lights of the street lamps and passing cars and blurring the hard edges of the buildings we passed.

Maggie kept looking at me as we hurried along, and I wondered what our designers had in mind when matching us as partners. She was my opposite, naïve, fun loving, silly, and now apparently obsessed with her appearance. Like so many women, she misjudged herself there. By current standards, she did run a few pounds overweight, but in my other manifestations I had visited cities and villages where bulky women were all the rage. Reubens put some of them on canvas, vibrant fleshy women, and in Mauretania men still want their wives rolling in layers of fat.

But Maggie wasn't fat. And she wasn't plain or ugly. Her designer had in fact taken pains to make her beautiful. She may have thought her nose a little long and pointed, and a mole dotted the left side of that firm neck, yet these were assets rather than liabilities. She was blessed with a wide and generous mouth, and her hazel eyes often glowed with pleasure like those of a happy cat. The combination of these assets, trumped by some ineffable magic—her voice maybe, the softness to her figure, her innocence—made me, and I suspect, other men want to be in her company, to laugh with her, to touch her.

On this particular evening, droplets of mist glittered like bits of silver in her golden, braided hair.

"I'm curious. You once called yourself a horse-and-buggy girl. Where did she go?"

"Just for tonight, Max, I've traded that rig in for a Ferrari."

She said nothing further until we reached Olive or Twist on Broadway. Once she did squeeze my hand, and when I looked at her, she grinned at me and waggled her eyebrows.

She looked, as I say, adorable.

The Olive or Twist was booming with noise, patrons, and dancers. It was a mixed crowd, young and old, some dressed almost formally, others wearing jeans and t-shirts and sporting tattoos. A middle-aged woman in a far corner who had charge of the music waved to us as we entered. Still grasping my hand, Maggie led me to the polished bar.

"I'd like a martini, please," she said to the man at the bar. "Very dry."

"I thought you weren't drinking."

"It's not for me. It's for you, Max. I hate to see you suffer." She gave me a grin, then added to the bartender: "And a soda water, please."

When he brought our drinks, Maggie insisted on paying and then directed me to a nearby table for two.

"Cheers," she said, and clicked her glass against mine.

"Cheers," I said. I sipped at my drink. The ice-cold concoction created a buzz in my mouth. "Excellent."

"Let me have a taste," Maggie said, and before I could stop her, she took the glass from my hand. I was certain she would gag or choke on the potent drink, but she closed her eyes, letting the gin rest in her mouth, and then swallowed. "Marvelous."

"I wonder if there's some chromosomal tendency toward alcoholism in your manifestation."

"I love it when you talk dirty, Max." She took a second taste and scooted the glass back across the table to me. "Cold and sharp. It makes me feel like the twenties."

"You are in your twenties."

"No, I mean the 1920s. Like Zelda and Scott Fitzgerald. There's something dangerous and sophisticated about a martini. Maybe it's why some people were so wild back then. The taste makes me want to shimmy or do the Charleston." She saluted me with her own glass of chaste soda water, drank, and then reached across the table to touch my hand. "Do you want to dance yet? Or do you dance?"

"No to the first question. Yes to the second." Holding her hand earlier that evening, I had the sensation of our flesh melting together, until I could no longer tell her fingers from mine. In an effort to keep this from happening again, I raised a question. "Practice is good, but do you really expect Emily to behave this way?"

"No, but you wanted us to set an example. If we're going dancing, we should look as if we've danced together."

"John doesn't strike me as a dancer of any sort."

"Well, someone must dance. Otherwise, why would she have suggested it?"

"She's a woman."

How a nice soft hand can turn to ice in a wink is surely one of the miracles of nature. "What's that supposed to mean?"

"Maybe she didn't consult John. Maybe she just wanted to go dancing."

"Are you still spouting that chauvinistic garbage? Ain't I a woman?"

"Harriet Tubman. Really? You're quoting Harriet Tubman?"

"So?"

"No," I said. "You're not a woman, and you know it. No more than I'm a man."

She looked at me, her cat's eyes wide, her lips crooked in a smile, and that look split me in half. The spirit in me remained reasonable, detached, neutral, but the man I was, my manifestation, wanted nothing more than to lean forward and kiss that smile.

Just then someone tapped my shoulder. An elderly woman, wrinkled, hair grey as ashes, loomed above me, leaning on a cane. She wore a print dress and on her mouth a bow of red lipstick. "Pardon my intrusion," she said. She propped the cane against the table and put one hand on each of our shoulders. "My party wants to go now"—she nodded to the door, where three other women and a man stood waiting for her—"but I had to tell you what fun I've had watching you two these last few minutes. You remind me so much of me and my Dan. He's been gone fifteen years now, but seeing you helped bring him back to me. You have the electricity we once had."

"That's so sweet," Maggie said. She had reached up to touch the woman's hand.

"There's something special between you," the woman said. She pointed with her chin toward her companions while looking at the two of us. "They don't see it, but I do. Love—it's pouring out of you. You have a certain glow."

"That's so sweet of you," Maggie said again.

"Respect. Mutual respect. That's what Dan and I discovered was the key. Forty-seven years of happiness based on love and respect."

Maggie's wide eyes glittered with tears.

"God bless the two of you," the woman said, and left to join her friends.

"Well," Maggie said, picking up a cocktail napkin to dab at the corners of her eyes. "Wasn't that just the sweetest thing?"

I refrained from commenting on her limited vocabulary. The old woman's interruption was, after all, sweet. "Do you think something's showing through? Are we supposed to be this affectionate? Maybe she noticed because we're not really human. Maybe she—"

"Oh, Max, that's not it. That's not it at all. Why don't we practice some dancing?"

We were awkward together our first couple of swing dances. My manifestation tended toward a conservative style while Maggie wanted to be slung all over the floor. Soon our bodies adjusted and compromised, and we were dancing on a par with the other couples. Then the DJ played "Up On The Roof," and we swayed together. Maggie nestled her face against my shoulder, humming the tune. Her hair smelled of flowers and spring, doubtless the result of one of the hundreds of shampoos available these days.

Holding her close revived the sensation of the touch of her fingers in the theater. Something was happening to me that had never occurred on any other assignment, something new and frightening, and sooner or later I would need to acknowledge my attraction and tell Maggie I found her alluring. I even wondered whether the controllers might not pull me off the assignment. We aren't supposed to have these feelings, and the sensation disturbed me, but at the same time all I wanted to do was to hold her even closer, a physical impossibility unless we removed our clothing.

At the end of the song, Maggie continued to rest her head on my shoulder and I wondered if she was tired. Just as she pulled away, the DJ announced, "Time to mix it up, folks, time to mix it up," which was the signal, understood by all the regulars, to find a different partner. Near us a tall man in his mid-forties with wavy hair and a deep tan dropped his partner's hands as if scalded, marched up to us, and asked Maggie to dance. Looking past him, I noted that the woman he'd left was either weary of dancing or of his company, for she went at once to her table of friends.

As I was left alone on the floor, I returned to our table, sat, nursed my drink, and watched the dancers. In my many visitations, I had seen all sorts of dances: the celebrated tribal dances of the Kikuyu, the colorful mazurka of the Poles, the minuet, a fabulous waltz in, of all places, Abilene, Texas. Women dance, I had observed, for pleasure and entertainment, while men dance mostly for pleasure and sex.

The latter was the case for the tall man. During the first dance, a fast swing number, he was fairly discrete, though I did note that he managed to brush his hands against Maggie's breasts once when reaching to twirl her and that he kept staring intently at those same breasts.

During the slow dance that followed he dropped all pretenses. They began with a wall of air between them, but then he pulled Maggie close to him, locking her against his barrel chest, and the hand in the small of her back slipped down six inches. He whispered something in her ear, and she tried pushing him away, but he laughed and held her close and whispered again, pawing at her with the straying hand. Maggie jerked her head back, and a look of disgust and fear twisted across her face.

The tap on the man's shoulder interrupted his assault. "What do you want?" he said to me, still clutching Maggie.

"I'm cutting in."

"No, now's not the right time. After this dance."

"Now," I said, striving to sound as civil as possible, "strikes me as the best possible time."

He stopped and faced me. "What's up with you? Don't you understand the word no?"

He was a good fifteen years older than I, a beer-swilling bully running to fat and given to bluster. The dancing had dampened his forehead with sheen of perspiration.

"I understand the word no," I said. "I wonder if you understand a tap on the shoulder."

"Look, bubba, I'm going to finish this dance."

"No, you're not."

He tried glaring at me, but even then I knew I had him. "If you can't agree with my proposition or if you don't understand me," I said, "we could carry the discussion outside. I have a different sort of dictionary there and we could look up a few words together."

He tried the glare for a second longer, then dropped Maggie's hand and sauntered off to the bar without looking back. As I took Maggie's hand, the music shifted to a faster pace.

"Had enough for a while?"

"Yes."

At the table she took several gulps of her soda water while looking at me over the rim of her glass.

"What is it?"

"Thank you for rescuing me, Max."

"I'm supposed to rescue you. It's what one does when courting or going out or dating or whatever it is we're doing."

We needed some definitions. When words lose their meanings, chaos ensues. In our case, the words defining our relationship had become as muddled as ditch-water.

"He wouldn't let go of me."

"He was drunk. And mean in the bargain. I hope I didn't break some tenet of feminism defending you."

She put her hand on my knee.

We stayed another hour, dancing or watching the others dance. We spoke only a little, but touched each other more naturally now. We held hands, we leaned into each other dancing. Our evening of training and practice was a success.

It was almost midnight when we left the Olive or Twist and walked down the street until we came to the shadowy doorway of a clothing store where we might return to our natural state without causing alarm.

"Saturday, then?"

"We might want to meet beforehand. We could pop in on Emily and John, and then compare our findings." The truth was I wanted to see her alone again. "Mutual reports might be helpful."

"Friday?"

"That would work."

"How about noon? There's a Mass at Saint Lawrence and we could go for some lunch afterwards."

"Do you want to be on the altar with the others? Or—"

"No, Max," Maggie said. "I want to sit with you at Mass."

Chapter Six

Individual report: Emily Hoffman: M. Hart.

Thursday evening was spent observing my client, Emily Hoffman. Just before six o'clock, she returned from a teaching workshop at the school. She immediately opened her computer and checked her email. With an audible sigh she went to the kitchen, took the remains of an artichoke salad from the refrigerator, opened a diet cola, and returned to the apartment's one large room where she watched a rerun of *Frasier* while she ate supper. Twice during that supper she rose to look again at her computer.

After her meal she read for half an hour or so from a book on teaching grammar and phonics to the very young. She checked her computer once more, then changed into jogging shorts and a t-shirt, and went for half an hour's run in the twilight. On her return she drank a large glass of water, performed ten minutes of crunches, squats, and other exercises in front of the television, tidied the kitchen, and dusted the two shelves of books in the living room, all the while eyeing her computer.

When she finally gave way to temptation and hit the keys again, she had her reward. The lowering of her shoulders and a long whoosh of breath told me that she had heard from John. Over her shoulders I read his note, which was quite long and which gave an account of his day—astonishingly, John possessed that gift for detail prized by so many women and spurned by so many men. He told of an older woman who had beaten on the top of the glass counter of the pharmacy to attract his attention, a child who had overturned a display of sunglasses, a man who had whispered of the need for a salve after developing a rash in his crotch.

For two entire paragraphs he rummaged around his thoughts and words trying to describe how he felt about her, how he considered himself lucky to count her as a new friend, how attractive she was in appearance and personality, and how much he was anticipating the weekend with her. I was heartened to see that they would spend Friday evening at the movies and that they planned to meet for supper on Saturday before joining us at the Olive or Twist for dancing. Emily read the note, laughed at his anecdotes about the oddities of patients he had encountered that day, but then frowned and began hammering out a response, pausing from time to time to edit what she had written or to think of a pleasing turn of phrase.

I left without reading her response. She is clearly counting the hours until she might see him again. As for myself, I look forward to seeing Max tomorrow and reporting this instance of our mutual success.

Private report: M. Hart

Max arrived just before the bell announced the entrance of the priest.

He was dressed in a light blue shirt and khaki trousers with a brown belt and brown shoes. He wore no tie, but in spite of the warm day, he had put on a blue blazer. He dropped a paper bag on the pew and joined in the opening prayers.

This weekday Mass at first filled me with a sense of tranquility. The spacious church engulfed the few communicants, hugging us in silence and contemplative peace. Max and I spoke the prayers along with the others, made the responses to the priests, listened to the Gospel and the homily. As a spirit, I had attended tens of thousands of masses at the altar, standing with Him at the re-creation of Calvary, singing countless hymns of praise and glory, thanksgiving and gratitude.

Never while attending those Masses had I been aware of any sensation other than His holy presence. Never had I felt distracted; indeed, I could not even imagine the sensation. When I sang the hymns of praise, when I joined the prayers of thanksgiving, when I glorified, adored, and worshipped the bread become flesh, I was not only focused on the altar, but was also a part of everything happening there and the tremendous gift His sacrifice had brought to all humankind.

Now, for the first time, an intruder had entered this domain, an invader who corrupted the sanctity of the Mass, a trespasser who jangled the music, jumbled the prayers, and jarred the spirit. I had invited Max to Mass as a test, and I had failed the test. I was aware of the sacrifice at the altar, the offering of His Body and Blood, but my immersion in all this beauty and truth was compromised by the body and blood beside me and by the body and blood I inhabited. I keenly felt the moment when the priest on the altar stared at the Host and declared, "This is my body, which is given up for you," but at the same moment the spirit-man beside me thrust himself into my thoughts and feelings.

I was aware of Max. There is no better way to put it. I was aware of him, and that awareness terrified me. *Max* terrified me.

I had heard many tales of those who had gone on assignments, overseeing the care of souls and tending to their multitude of woes. A man whose hands were eaten away by leprosy, a mother whose five children terrorists had nailed to trees, children whose mothers were savagely raped, lovers abandoned and encamped on the cliffs of self-destruction, souls male and female who had cried out for love and light, only to be given disdain and darkness: I had heard these stories of the suffering and agony of human creatures, and had felt for them admiration, sorrow, and pity.

On most of our assignments humans never hear or see their guardians—at least, not in the flesh. These guardians make themselves known through the energies of the One who sent them. That energy, which exists beyond all human knowledge, gives those suffering souls faith, hope, and love, and offers comfort and direction in times of great adversity. Thousands of times a day all around this fallen Eden guardians give support to those assigned to them, mainly through prayer. Only on special occasions does the Generator of Love bid his spirits to take on the flesh of one of these creatures, to walk and breath in this all too heavy flesh.

From time to time, rumors have come to us of one of our own becoming too strongly attracted to a human creature, of wanting to remain with that creature when the assignment and manifestation were complete. These tidings were practically impossible to believe, for who in our realm would ever exchange perfect happiness to dwell in such a place of shades and sighs?

Yet here I was on my first assignment, manifested as a female human and attracted to the man kneeling beside me. No—not a man, but a creature like me. And this—this circumstance I had never heard of. No one of all the choirs had even hinted of this possibility, and I didn't understand what was happening or what to do. Was I attracted to Max because we were of the same nature? Was it his spirit and wit that so strongly drew me to him? His flesh? (After all, he is striking in appearance, and he knows it and doesn't care, or doesn't seem to care, which only makes him even more attractive). And how can flesh appear as handsome or beautiful, ugly or pathetic, to a creature such as I, a creature composed of pure spirit and so beyond material values?

And He knew. He knows. Of that I was absolutely certain, for He is omniscient and sees into the hearts and minds of every one of His creatures. He knew, yet here I was in this church, sitting beside Max, manifested, still on my mission. Given my feelings for Max, why was I permitted to remain a manifestation? Was I a part of some divine experiment? If so, was I a success or a failure?

"Max?"

He turned slightly toward me, startled by my intrusion.

"Can I take communion?" I whispered.

I so wanted to receive communion. We who live in the Light feel the energy pouring from the altar, but to experience that power directly, to ingest the transformed bread and wine, excited me.

"Why not?" he whispered back. The fervency in his voice told me that he too was excited by the prospect of what was about to happen.

"The Sky Bar. The drinking. I was drunk. I sinned." I choked back tears saying these words.

"No sin," Max said. He took my hand. "It wasn't intentional. There was no sin."

And so we joined the communicants shuffling toward the altar. Max went ahead of me, probably wanting to show me the proper way to receive this great gift. He genuflected, made the sign of the cross, responded "Amen" when the old priest murmured "Body of Christ," tilted his head back, and received the host. When I followed suit and the priest placed the Body on my tongue, the joy that infused my own body and mind were so powerful that I felt radiant with an inner light. How did humans endure such a great gift? How could they partake of Him so casually? And why were so few here to receive Him?

General report: M. Lamb: An evening with John Flyte

"Religion," wrote the father of communism, "is the opiate of the masses."

Poor old Karl. Even when he wrote that famous tag, the words had grown mossy with age. The opiate of religion was even then being replaced by politics, sex, and sports. Movies, television, football, baseball, basketball, golf, the Internet, online games, online pornography: Americans spend hours every day chasing these amusements. While they may derive some good these pleasures—sports, for example, can teach morality and enhance contemplation—such entertainments can cause participants to neglect all other obligations, ranging from their spouses and children to public affairs. Never before in human history have so many been entertained by so much.

When I arrived at John's house this evening for a beer and a visit, I found him playing golf on his Wii in the living room. He wiped his face with a hand-towel, returned to the television to switch off the machine, and cracked open two Heinekens. "You play?" he asked, gesturing to the machine after we'd seated ourselves on the sofa.

"Wii?"

"No. Golf."

"I'm afraid not."

"I played a lot growing up. Golf was about all my dad did except for work. I don't get out much anymore—golf takes too long, and I became bored with it—but I like to get on the machine and play when I get frustrated."

"From what I understand, golf itself is an exercise in frustration."

"True."

"So why are you frustrated right now?"

"It's Emily. I emailed her this evening and asked her out for tomorrow night—I mean, it's Friday, so I assumed she'd want to get together—but she wrote back saying she'd made plans with two teachers from her school. She said I should have asked her earlier."

"Ah. The Wednesday rule."

"Wednesday rule?"

"Wednesday's the cut-off point for many women. If you don't call and make a date by that point, you indicate a lack of interest."

"She could always ask me out. It's the twenty-first century. Women's lib and all that."

I ignored his petulant tone. "True. But most women still enjoy being called. Pursuit by men remains the norm."

"And then she wondered why I hadn't texted or called her yesterday. Why would I do that? I didn't have anything to say."

"Probably not, but those little things mean a lot to women like Emily. They make her feel secure and wanted. And you don't need to say much. Just say hi. Ask her what she's doing. Tell her a joke. Let her hear from you."

"That's such a pain."

"Do you like her?"

"Hell, yes. I like her. She's different from any woman I've ever known."

I pushed aside his curse and his mistaken belief that Emily was unique. Several of the women he had known undoubtedly exhibited the same desires and might have exerted a similar attraction, but he'd been too blind to see them, too wrapped up in himself and his own interests to pay attention to them. "So is she mad at you?"

"I guess." He slumped back on the sofa, dangling his beer bottle from two fingers. "I will never understand women."

"They're a mystery all right, but I'm not sure we're supposed to understand them as much as we are to love them."

"Do you and Maggie fight sometimes?"

His question made me think of my own quarrels with Maggie when we'd first begun working together. That initial prickliness was mostly gone, and I found myself thinking of the happiness she brought me whenever we met. Shame at my former irritation with her washed through me. "We've fought. Verbal dueling, mostly."

"So how do you make up?"

"In different ways." The shame deepened as I considered how coldly I had first treated Maggie, how I had scorned her as an amateur, transformed her into a second-rate sidekick. "Look," I said, "you've made a mistake, but you can easily erase it. You need to respond to her this evening. Don't let her brood."

"You think I should call her? She was really upset. I could tell—"

"No, don't call her. Go see her. Do you think she's home?"

"She said she planned to do some laundry and then read this evening."

"Go see her. Stop first at the grocery store and buy her some flowers. Bring a bottle of wine. It's warm outside—better make it a chardonnay, if you can find something decent chilled."

"Flowers?"

He was as uninformed about women as a four-year-old about higher mathematics. My admiration for Emily and her kindergarten teaching jumped another few notches. Concealing my exasperation, I said: "Buy her a small bouquet of flowers. Not roses—too strong a statement. Just a spring mix. You might consider adding some dark chocolate to your purchases. Don't buy a bar of the chocolate—buy a box."

"Yeah," he said. "I can do that. But what do I say?"

"You apologize. You ring the doorbell, and when she answers she'll see you standing there with the flowers in hand and she'll know you've come to apologize. But you say the words anyway. And you tell her the truth—that you are new at this part of a relationship and that you're still learning."

"She'll think I'm stupid."

"No, she'll think you're sweet. She'll be touched by your confession and your honesty."

"What if she has a girlfriend over?"

"All the better. Emily will have a witness to your contrition and your goodness. They will probably analyze you for hours when they meet again, but I'm reasonably certain you'll receive high marks. It helps to have her friends in your corner."

His brow unfurrowed itself, and he smiled. "I suppose I'd better shower and head out."

"Yes."

"I'm sorry the evening didn't work out. We'll do it again sometime."

"Of course."

Note to self: Buy some flowers and chocolate for Maggie.

Chapter Seven

General Report: M. Hart: An Evening with Emily Hoffman

When I arrived, Emily had just finished eating a supper of a Tex-Mex chicken soup, a concoction learned from her mother. She had gone running while the soup simmered on the stove and was still decked out in grey gym shorts and a pink t-shirt. Though from past meetings I had apprehended her trim build, this was the first time I'd seen her in shorts and a t-shirt, and her appearance surprised me. She was longer-legged than I'd imagined. Perhaps I noticed her legs because of a poll I'd read online taken among English women regarding their appearance in which, when asked which physical feature they might change about themselves, they reported in large numbers wanting to lengthen their lower extremities. Emily's own legs were, I thought, beyond criticism.

"I made some herbal iced tea earlier," she said. "Raspberry. Would you care for a glass?"

"Thank you. That would be nice."

While she poured the tea in the kitchen, I checked out the living room. Emily's laptop and some papers were on the dining room table. On the arm of the sofa a Catholic magazine, *Magnificat,* lay atop Jay Parini's *The Art of Teaching.* The headband she had worn while running and a framed photograph of her family sat on a trunk doing double duty as an end table. Everything was tidy, clean, dusted.

"I'm glad you're here," Emily said, bringing in the two icy glasses of tea. We sat on the sofa. "I could use a sounding board, if you don't mind."

"Not at all."

"It's John. He called me about an hour ago to ask me out for tomorrow evening. I told him I already had plans. I could tell he was angry, but it's not right to call at the last minute. We've just started seeing each other and I don't want to be taken for granted. Now I'm wondering if I did the right thing?"

"Do you have plans?"

She nodded. "Sort of. One of the teachers invited some of the staff to her house for a cookout. I told her no when she invited me, but when John didn't call, I called her back and told her I'd like to come after all."

"You did the right thing. He can't expect you to wait around for him. He needs to plan ahead."

Suddenly I thought of Max. Would he behave so inconsiderately if he were truly human? Probably. He possessed manners and polish, but he also had enough arrogance for any five men. He might easily have behaved as stupidly as John.

"Yes, but that's not all. I asked him why he hadn't texted me or phoned me very much this week. When we first met, he texted every day, sometimes three and four times, and he called me every night. But since last weekend when we last saw each other he's cut way back. I can't tell if he still likes me."

"Emily, I'm sure he likes you. He wouldn't have asked you out otherwise."

"Then why the loss of interest?"

"Well, maybe he really has started taking you for granted."

"But we've only gone out five times. Six if you count the night we met."

I hesitated to explain that, given John's track record, six dates meant you were on the way to a long-term relationship. John, I wanted to tell her, was a sprinter. Until now John had been good at sprinting, with the finish line being the bedroom. He was handsome, exuded a certain charm, and practiced a respectable and lucrative profession, all of which attracted women, but he'd spent his dating time trying to get his companion into the sack rather than getting to know her.

Now Emily had come along, stirring up feelings that had lain dormant inside him his entire life. She was a long-distance runner, and he didn't yet have the stamina to match hers. She sat facing me on the other side of the sofa, her long legs crossed, her scarlet hair in a ponytail with loose strands about her face. She looked so sad and woebegone that had John suddenly appeared I might have dashed my tea into his stupefied face. What was wrong with men? Again I thought of Max and again I wondered: if he were a real man, would he behave so ignorantly and selfishly? Probably so, I decided. He wouldn't behave as immaturely as John, or be as befuddled by a woman's reaction, but I had no doubt he might have treated a woman as John had treated Emily.

Then another thought occurred to me. How had I treated Max? How was I supposed to treat him? Even in this careless age, which was smothering decency, goodness, and true love with a blanket of sex and pornography, many boys were still taught to open doors for women, to treat women with more diffidence than they showed to their male friends, to refrain from hitting them. Of course, many men either never learned or else broke these rules. Certainly millions of women claimed physical or emotional abuse, and millions more deplored the lack of manners in males.

Yet what of the women themselves? What were they taught about boys when they were girls? Were none of them guilty of emotional abuse, of hitting a man, of demeaning him? Where was their loyalty to men? What lessons did their parents teach them in the treatment of males? Women demanded respect and understanding from men, but what did they extend in return?

It was all very puzzling.

"What is it you like about John?" I asked, truly curious now.

"Well, there are the usual things most women would like. He's good-looking. He has a nice job. He's fun. But there's more. John's all bluster on the surface, but I think he's really tender and sweet when you get to know him. And he's vulnerable too—I don't like that word, but it's all I can think of right now. He's easily hurt. He doesn't show it unless you watch his eyes. From what he's told me about his parents, I think he learned early on to hide some of his feelings. Sometimes he's like a little boy. I know that's a silly reason to like him, but he's sweet. I think the two of us would fit well together if he'd wake up and look at me and treat me the right way."

"How do you fit together?"

"Well, John's outgoing and I tend to be shy. He's exciting and likes to do all sorts of things, physical activities, whereas I like to stay home and read or garden. If we were together, maybe he'd liven up my life and maybe I'd calm him down. He'd stand up for me, I think, and I can help him grow up. We don't share the same religious faith—I'm not sure he has much faith—but maybe he could learn that from me. He already seems interested."

"Those all sound like positives."

"And he doesn't do drugs and he doesn't like drinking very much—I think it has something to do with his parents—and I'm the same way. He told me he really got tired of the parties and binge drinking in college."

At the mention of alcohol and inebriation I reddened. "He must not think much of me then. Not after the Sky Bar."

"I didn't mean you," Emily said quickly. "I wasn't even thinking of you. In fact, he thought you were cute the way you kept bumping Max." She titled her glass and sucked an ice cube into her mouth. "What do you think I should do?"

"The ball's in his court. I'd wait a while and see what he does with it."

"So I shouldn't call him?"

"Have you been calling him?"

"Only a couple of times."

"Then I'd wait. It wasn't as if you told him not to call. You just explained you wanted to hear from him more often."

"Do you call Max sometimes?"

"Oh, yes. But that's different. Max and I have known each other much longer. And there's an understanding between us."

"What do you mean? What sort of an understanding?"

"What I said at the Arboretum. We both know we're going to be married to each other someday."

"You've talked about it? He's asked you?"

"No. But we both know it. The understanding is there."

She had just started asking me questions about my relationship with Max—how long we'd known each other, how we'd met, what attracted me to him—when there was a knock at her door.

It was John.

Emily stepped away from the doorway when she saw him, and he followed her inside, stopping when he became aware of me on the sofa. He looked as if he'd come straight from a shower—his hair was damp—and he was carrying a bouquet of flowers, a large box of chocolates, and a bottle of chardonnay.

"Hello John."

He jerked his head in my direction, "Maggie," and turned again to Emily, looking clumsy and alien in her apartment. He glanced at her legs. "I've never seen you in shorts before."

What a bozo.

"I just got back from a run and then Maggie dropped by."

John nodded again for no apparent reason. "I've brought you some flowers," he said, holding the plastic-wrapped bouquet stiff-armed toward Emily like one of her kindergarteners. From where I sat I could see the price tag on the side of the flowers.

Emily took the flowers from him and smelled them. "They're nice. I'll get a vase and put them on the dining room table."

"Chocolates, too," John said, extending the chocolates stiff-armed. "Dark."

"One of my favorites," Emily said, taking the box from him.

There was a short silence, and then John drew himself even straighter, blushing. "I should have called you about tomorrow night. I'm sorry I didn't."

"Apology accepted. Come on—you can help me with the vase."

"If you have the time, I thought we could share a glass of wine."

"Want some wine, Maggie?" Emily asked. She turned to me, blushing a little and smiling.

"No, I'd better run," I said.

"You don't need to leave on my account," John said.

"No, I have some errands," I said. "Those flowers are pretty, by the way."

"Thanks."

As I left, I could hear them from the staircase, talking and laughing with each other.

Chapter Eight

General file: Recording: Margaret and Maximilian

Margaret: You do realize those tubes are full of cast-off parts, don't you?

Maximilian: When in Rome…and whatever they're made of, they're delectable. The chili and slaw are delicious too. A little sloppy, it's true, but nectar of the gods, as the old adage goes. Much more tasty than that measly cheese sandwich you're eating.

Margaret: It's Friday. The traditional go meatless.

Maximilian: The Church no longer requires that.

Margaret: No, but it does require some act of penance on Fridays.

Maximilian: Does eating a hot dog in the presence of a food-Nazi count as penance?

Margaret: Ha-ha. Very funny. Here—lean toward me. There. You have a blob of mustard in the corner of your mouth.

Maximilian: Sure you don't want a bite?

Margaret: Yuck. I shudder at the thought. Besides, I'd feel guilty for stealing even a tiny part of your pleasure.

Maximilian: Did you know your eyes crinkle when you smile? No—don't look worried. They crinkle then too.

Margaret: Really? Do you think I'll have wrinkles when I'm old?

Maximilian: Hardly a worry, is it? Unless our project with John and Emily takes twenty years or so of our time. But wrinkles or not, you'd be a beautiful old lady.

Margaret: A compliment! I'm flattered.

Maximilian: Credit the hot dog. Do you know that I once ate cooked dog meat?

Margaret: That's disgusting.

Maximilian: Quite so. I was in what is today called Indonesia and I didn't know what I was eating until I'd had my fill. I thought I might be sick, but then decided to take the whole thing philosophically. The dog was already part of the meal, and the meal was already a part of me. And to be honest, the spices made for a tasty dish.

Margaret: Yuck again. Let's try a different topic. You received the report on Emily?

Maximilian: It sounds promising.

Margaret: You didn't send me one on John.

Maximilian: It seemed less complicated to describe John verbally. To begin, he's quite a gamester, our boy John. One room of his house could pass as an arcade. He has video games, a dart board, a pool table, a flat-screen television set the size of a buffalo hide, a Wii for the television, a bookcase filled with movies, a table used solely for poker, and a wet bar. In the double garage, in addition to his car, are a Ping-Pong table, a mountain bike, and an entire corner piled high with all sorts of sports equipment. He's created the fantasy land of a fourteen-year-old.

Margaret: Very different from Emily's place.

Maximilian: Very different indeed. And very expensive.

Margaret: His family has money?

Maximilian: They do. And pharmacists are well paid. At any rate, he is clearly smitten with Emily. Following his make-up visit with her, I observed him unseen after he had returned to his house. He was playing golf on the Wii, swinging away and muttering curses whenever he missed a shot. After the completion of each hole he would glance at his laptop, mutter again, and then resume the game. It was clear he wanted to write Emily, but was unsure of what to say. Finally he sat at the desk with a beer at his elbow and began typing out a letter to her. When he clicked "send," he sat looking at the machine, then stood and went into the kitchen and microwaved a mini pizza. He went back to the computer and shouted "Yes!" when he saw Emily's response. He immediately invited her to do some instant messaging.

Margaret: How'd that go?

Maximilian: It was sweet, watching him, though if I were unaware of the circumstances I might assume he was a lunatic. Their messages zipped back and forth, and he was smiling—he even laughed aloud a few times—and was banging away on the keys like some sort of half-crazed, joyful Beethoven. This went on for nearly two hours. Mostly, the two of them discussed their childhoods and their college days. John needs some pointers in grammar and syntax, but I doubt Emily minded, as his enthusiasm for her shone in every line. From what he wrote, he seems especially taken by her eyes.

Margaret: I am happy to report she has ditched the black glasses.

Maximilian: So tonight we leave them to their own devices and then tomorrow meet them at the Olive or Twist.

Margaret: Correct. And then we report how they're getting along together. I do hope all goes well. Knowing the goal of this exercise would certainly help. It seems a lot of trouble just to get the two of them together. And I keep wondering why we're left here. We've gotten them together.

Maximilian: No point in bringing that up again. By the way, that sundress suits you. The peach color in the pattern puts roses in your complexion. And you're carrying that same scent today. You smell of sunshine and wildflowers. Is it shampoo?

Margaret: Do you like it?

Maximilian: Immensely.

Margaret: It's a perfume. You look nice too, Max. You have a predilection, it seems, for khaki trousers.

Maximilian: They're what I'm given. Khaki must fit the personality of an attorney on vacation. In the courtroom I would wear dark suits, a red tie, and gunboat shoes, black wingtips, a standard uniform for screwing the opposition to the wall.

Margaret: You would be intimidating in a courtroom. You're very well-spoken.

Maximilian: Thank you, I think.

Margaret: I intended a compliment.

Maximilian: Shall we take a stroll? We could wander down to Pack Square, sit on a bench, and watch the children playing in the fountain.

Margaret: I suppose we should hold hands, shouldn't we?

Maximilian: Of course.

File: Recording Continued: Margaret and Maximilian

Margaret: I love how the sun splashes on the water, how it feels on my face.

Maximilian: That sun has already given your cheeks some more pink roses.

Margaret: Am I too pale?

Maximilian: Not at all. Now that little girl over there—she's pale. She'll burn if her mother doesn't quit reading that book and put some sunscreen on her. It's a noisy crew, isn't it? Must be some sort of day care group. I'll bet that water feels good.

Margaret: Should we kick off our shoes and go wading?

Maximilian: Let's wait a few minutes. We've just sat.

Margaret: I like the way your fingers feel when you touch my face that way. Would we have children, do you think, Max?

Maximilian: Half a dozen. Three boys and three girls. We'd name the boys Jacob, Michael, and Jeremy, and the girls Mary, Katherine, and Laura. We'd call the girls by their full names, but the boys would go by Jake, Mike, and Jer. Traditional names, yes, but I prefer to avoid names like August or Summer or Carter or Buckhead.

Margaret: Have you ever known someone named Buckhead?

Maximilian: No, it's a posh neighborhood in Atlanta, Georgia. But given the propensity these days for exotic names, you can be sure someone is named Buckhead.

Margaret: Wouldn't we name one of the boys Maximilian?

Maximilian: Heavens, no. Maximilian Junior is awful, and Maximilian the Second sounds as if he's next in line as a Hapsburg Emperor. But we could name one of the girls Margaret.

Margaret: Not unless we can call her Maggie. But that might make telephone calls confusing.

Maximilian: You feel warm. You still want to kick off those shoes?

Margaret: I was hoping you'd ask.

Maximilian: Please leave on that silver ankle bracelet.

Margaret: Do you like it?

Maximilian: It's very attractive.

Margaret: It came with today's outfit. What do you like about it?

Maximilian: It gives you the look of a slave or a queen—I can't decide which. Maybe both.

Margaret: Ummm.

Maximilian: What is it?

Margaret: When you touch my cheeks and throat that way, I feel the touch deep inside. Do you suppose humans feel that way, too?

Maximilian: They do. A lot of them, anyway. Do you know, I would very much like to kiss you. We haven't practiced that enough, I think.

Margaret: Remember that first smooch in the Sky Bar. How awful I was that night.

Maximilian: I prefer to think of you as enthusiastic. Would you mind?

Margaret: About the kiss, you mean?

Maximilian: Yes.

Margaret: No.

Maximilian: Well?

Margaret: Well what?

Maximilian: Was it nice for you?

Margaret: "Nice" might be the understatement of the century. It made me go all weak inside. I thought of sunshine right after a rain, and fields of poppies, and ocean waves running against the sand. How about you? What were you thinking when we kissed?

Maximilian: A thousand champagne bottles popping all at once with fireworks exploding overhead.

Margaret: Your lips taste like peppermint.

Maximilian: One of the mints from the restaurant's checkout counter. I suppose it's to conceal the odor of the frankfurters and chili.

Margaret: Max, I have a confession to make.

Maximilian: I'm not a priest.

Margaret: Very funny. No—you're definitely not a priest.

Maximilian: Well, confess away.

Margaret: Max, I like kissing you. I think I like it too much.

Maximilian: The sensation is mutual.

Margaret: May I ask you something?

Maximilian: Of course.

Margaret: Are we supposed to like it?

Maximilian: I don't know.

Margaret: But I thought with all your manifestations and all that kissing—I thought you would know.

Maximilian: You're back to the kissing again. You worry too much about that.

Margaret: Did you like it when you kissed all those other women?

Maximilian: Heavens—I'm not Catullus.

Margaret: Catullus?

Maximilian: A Roman poet who wrote to a woman, an adulteress, asking for thousands of kisses.

Margaret: Well, tell me, Max. When you kissed those women, did the kissing feel the way it does with me?

Maximilian: I don't remember it feeling this way.

Margaret: What about that gorgeous Irish woman?

Maximilian: She wasn't gorgeous. She was tragically beautiful. And I don't remember her because of the kiss. I remember her because of her grief. As to whether we're supposed to enjoy kissing each other, or even if we should be kissing each other, I can't answer you.

Margaret: Why not, Max?

Maximilian: Because I've never kissed another manifestation.

Margaret: Not one?

Maximilian: Never. And I've never heard of any manifestation kissing another manifestation. Never. So this kissing and all the sensations the kisses provoke is as new to me as it is to you.

Margaret: You're so worldly. I thought you would know.

Maximilian: Sorry, my dear. Not a clue.

Margaret: Are we supposed to enjoy it this much?

Maximilian: Not a clue.

Margaret: Should we try it again, Max? I may need just a little more practice. Besides, maybe it won't be the same this time. Maybe we'll be dull or boring.

Maximilian: Practice does indeed make perfect.

Margaret: I'm not sure I can kiss you and laugh at the same time.

Maximilian: Let's try. But first let's stop the recording.

Chapter Nine

Report: Public file: M. Lamb

For Saturday evening, the last day of May, we arranged to meet our other couple in Pack Square for supper and a stroll about town possibly followed either by dancing or a movie.

In order to offer him much-needed counsel, I arranged to get together with John before our date. He was unaware of the purpose of our meeting. He suggested meeting at a sports bar, but I resisted, telling him that I preferred to meet al fresco (I had to explain to him that this term meant "outside") and that I would bring some liquid stimulant, in this case two coffees from Starbucks and a pack of spearmint Tic-Tacs to remove the odor from our breath once we had finished the coffee. He arrived just as I finished stirring sugar and a creamer containing hazelnut into my cup.

"Coffee?"

"I hope you drink it."

"It keeps me going all day. I guess one more cup won't hurt anything."

He declined sugar and cream, and sipped at his cup. This park, which stood in front of the county courthouse, was where Maggie and I had last met. The fountain in which Maggie and I had waded squirted several thin jets of water over three children in bathing suits, but otherwise the hard angles and concrete of the park seemed designed to resist human beings. Suddenly, perhaps because Maggie wasn't present to distract me, the architecture struck me as odd. A park should enfold its visitors, offering them shade and refreshment in the middle of a city, but here the hard benches and weird, alien sculptures rebuffed this concept, serving more as a sparkling extension of the heat and buildings than a green oasis.

"Did you happen to catch the Braves game last night?" John asked me.

"No, I missed it, I'm afraid."

"Too bad. Santana pitched a heck of a game."

"I'm not much of a fan, sorry."

"No big deal. So, Max, did you want to talk about anything specific?"

"Not particularly."

"When you asked to get together, I thought you might want some advice. Something having to do with Maggie. Everything okay in that department?"

"All's well."

"Yeah, well, if you ever need advice, don't hesitate to ask. I've gone out with a fair number of women in my time."

"I'll keep that offer in mind."

"Women can be tough. I've tried all sorts of different strategies, but I can't figure them out. All that stuff about men being from Mars and women from Venus—I mean, I never read the book, but it's absolutely true, you know. We're different as night and day."

"What sort of strategies?"

"How's that?"

"You mentioned strategies. What do you mean?"

His face reddened. "Oh, you know. Strategies."

"Give me an example."

"Well, I've tried all sorts of things. Once I dated a woman who loved gardening and so I helped her with her yard work. I'd come home from the pharmacy and change my clothes and go to her house, and she'd have supper made and then we'd work in the yard for an hour or so, planting flowers and pulling weeds, and then we'd have a glass of wine and go to bed. I wanted her to like me for helping, and she did, but all that gardening got to be a headache—I'm really not into plants— so I broke it off.

"And then there was this secretary I met in the grocery store—that's a great place to meet women, Max, if you know how to swing it—who was into Zen and yoga and all that junk. To make her happy, I went with her to a few yoga classes at the Y, but that didn't go so hot. The last time we went to class, I fell asleep when the instructor was putting us through our relaxation exercises, and apparently I even snored. And she wanted more and more from me—she called me or texted me all the time, and she was always asking me what I was doing—and I couldn't keep up with all the communications and finally she broke it off because she said I didn't communicate well. At least, that's what she said. That one hurt. I was beginning to really like her."

"What about love?"

"Love? Whoa, that's a scary word, isn't it?"

"Terrifying, apparently."

"Max, Max, it's like the song says: 'What's love got to do with it?' I'm not sure I've ever been in love. Maybe once, back in high school, with this girl named Debbie Wooten. Anyway, I'm not sure I'd know what love is. I mean, I've heard about it, but I don't know that I'd recognize it. I didn't really have any great example growing up. My parents love each other, at least I think they do, they're still together, but they go their own ways and they never show each other much affection. How about you? Ever been in love?"

"Oh yes."

"Who was she?"

She was not a she; she was not a he; but how do you explain that you have always loved the Unnamable One? I had encountered numerous humans I loved, including John, but that was in the line of duty, so to speak. So I chose the way of the familiar.

"Is," I said.

"Is?"

"She's Maggie."

"You love her?"

"With all my spirit."

"So what's it like? What's it feel like?"

This was a good question, and I thought hard about it. What did being in love mean? Or more simply, what did love mean? How did it feel? What did love do to the interior self? How did love change us? I thought of the Creator, the Lover, the Heart and Soul of Love. Yet I found myself short of the mark in terms of an actual explanation, because every time I sought divine meanings for love my mind summoned up Maggie.

Finally, I began. "When you love someone, you put her needs and desires ahead of your own, and if the love is real, then that person does the same for you. You spend the rest of your life exploring that person, and even then love is a mystery. But you come to accept that mystery. No—not just accept. You come to love the mystery and so you love in spite of everything the world tells you and sometimes in spite of everything that happens to you. As a man, you know in your heart of hearts that whatever life throws at the two of you, betrayal or abandonment of the beloved is no longer part of any equation. And you know you would die for the woman you love."

"I've heard all those things."

"Yes," I said. "The usual clichés apply. But they are lived rather than spoken."

He considered my remarks for a minute in silence, his face intent, a schoolboy confronted with a tough lesson. "I've heard love can get in the way of sex."

"I wouldn't know."

"So it's not getting in the way?"

"We don't have sex. Not the way you mean."

John was as shocked as if I'd told him I'd murdered my father and married my mother. "No way!"

"No," I said. "No sex."

"What do other people think about that?"

"I wouldn't know, as I don't usually go around shouting out the details of my private life. Besides, why would I care what they thought of me regarding sex?"

"And Maggie's happy?"

"What do you mean by happy?"

"You know. She goes along with it?"

"We go along together. When one slips, the other stands fast."

"But why?"

"We want to bring a gift to our union."

"Marriage?"

"Yes."

"That's another word that terrifies me," John said, and the terror showed on his face. He looked like a boy facing a labyrinth inhabited by monsters. "I mean, I look at my parents' marriage and don't want to live that way."

"You'll live your own way. Take your parents as a negative example. Choose your own path."

"I don't know if I could do all the things marriage requires. I don't know if I could ever love someone that much."

"What about Emily?"

"Emily?"

"How do you see her?"

"She's the best thing that's happened to me in a long time. She's beautiful—at least I think so—on the inside and the outside. I don't want to lose her. I just don't know how to make her want me."

"It's not that difficult. Do your best to be your best. And love her."

"I don't know," he said. "Maybe I should read some books. You know, the self-help kind."

Books? For the love of all that's holy, I thought. "Maybe," I said. "But I think you should trust less in books and go with your heart. If you need examples, find people around you who know what love is and who practice it every day of their lives."

"I don't know many people like that."

Sometimes, as now, John was as Maggie described him: obtuse, dense, thick as a brick. "Sure you do. But sometimes we just need a new pair of eyes to see what's right in front of us."

John started to ask another question, but then his face lit up, and he stood and waved. Emily was walking toward him, smiling, and he walked to meet her. Maggie trailed behind her, waving to me.

We spent the remainder of the evening strolling the downtown and poking around stores, ending our visit with ice cream at the Marble Slab, where I finally had my mint chocolate chip.

Two scoops.

Chapter Ten

File: Private: Notes to myself: Maximilian

Something is amiss.

Whether Maggie and I, or I alone, have gone off track by accident or whether we are mice in some celestial laboratory is unclear. Whatever the case, we have stepped into a new land, a frontier country without maps. By nature, we are pure spirits, and when we inhabit, as we sometimes must, the frame of a human being, we do not experience emotions in the same way as a human. We may feel mercy, pity, peace, to quote Blake, but we do not experience the temptations of vice: gluttony, thievery, lust, and so on. We inhabit these bodies as we might rent a room in a Holiday Inn, as a place to lay our heads but certainly nothing to call home.

These boundaries have vanished. We've touched. We've held hands. We've hip-jiggled, as Maggie calls it. We've kissed. Manifestations don't do these things—not with other manifestations. We have no call, no need, no urge, yet Maggie and I have gone beyond the call, discovered a need, and felt an urge. Or, at least, I have. Judging from her reactions, I surmise that Maggie has leapt—or been flung—aboard the same boat.

I have fallen in love with her.

At least, I think I feel as humans feel when they fall in love.

There—it is recorded, a confession to myself and to the One who knows all hearts, who knows every blade of grass in every field and every grain of sand on every beach, who reads the human heart and the celestial spirits as easily as a university professor might read "Jack and Jill". The way Maggie crinkles her nose against the sun, the modulations of her merry voice, the peal of her laughter, the way she moves when she walks, as if she were dancing, her soft kisses, her endearing clumsiness, even that bracelet against her ankle: these accouterments rattle my heart. What is it about the union of lips, two labra meeting together, a biological conjunction of tissue, nerve, and blood, that make the heart race, reduce the mind to pudding, and so overwhelm the emotions that one is compelled to close the eyes?

Our future meetings fill me with yearning and trepidation. We cannot possibly feel this way—it is beyond the experience of creatures like us—and yet here it is, the flame of human love in a creature not human. Yesterday when we kissed, and then kissed again, and then again and again, I kept thinking the emotion would burn itself out by our repetition and practice; I was certain the flames would diminish to smoldering embers and then die to cold ash, yet the opposite occurred. With each kiss, Maggie opened more and more to me, like a morning glory struck by the sun. When her lips parted, that warmth and openness drew me into her until I felt as if I was sliding down a chute into her heart. Once, breaking away, she murmured my name, "Max, oh Max," and those three syllables blazed like medallions she'd hung in the air.

What to do? Flesh is mortal. Flesh dies. And before it passes to dust, that same flesh so often fails the spirit, and vice-versa. It's no wonder human beings, men and women of all ages, fall into such a tangle when they encounter love and romance. Many of them attempt to live by reason, an excellent tool when investing in the stock market, conducting surgeries, constructing dams and power plants, crowning a tooth, sending astronauts into space, building cars, and performing that host of other tasks human beings generally do so well. But reason can carry one only so far into the heart, and then, as the blessed philosopher Blaise Pascal wrote, "Le coeur a ses raisons que le raison ne connait pas." The heart has its reasons which reason cannot know.

Only some humans truly understand how to love another human. The rest are bumbling amateurs driven by jealousy, greed, power, desire, and lust. Some want to shape the beloved in their own image; some mistake the perspiration of physical passion for the waters of love; some—many, in fact—set up their beloved as a deity, and suffer the consequent disappointments when flesh proves flesh.

So many humans fail to comprehend the nexus between love and responsibility. (One irony of the present age: the best human examination of this nexus was offered by an aging celibate, now in harmony with the One, in his collection of writings, *Love And Responsibility*). To love truly and well means taking responsibility for the beloved. To this current age of debacle and confusion, the idea of responsibility, also called duty, seems foreign. Duty itself has become onerous, a weight, a barricade to the fulfillment of the self, when in reality duty offers the best means of self-fulfillment.

Enough of philosophy. I remind myself here of my identity. My created state is as a spirit without flesh. I am low on the totem pole of creatures sharing this same state. I belong to that hierarchical order, called a choir by some human beings, which is closest to men and women in spirit, and whose members often act as intermediaries, watchers, messengers, and guardians. Besides serving as guardian to scores of human beings, I have carried out several hundred special missions such as this one. Always I have performed to the letter my duties; never have I varied one jot from my assignments.

Until now. *Until now.*

Am I, unbeknownst to myself, in rebellion? Have I become one of those who from pride demands that my will be done, and not His will? Or is my attraction for Maggie pre-ordained? Or is some other elementary force at play here?

Chapter Eleven

General Report: Margaret

Early June, and the four of us had just returned from Sunday Mass for a brunch at Emily's house. She had prepared everything before meeting us at the Basilica: a sausage-and-egg casserole, biscuits, strawberries and blueberries, orange juice and coffee. We ate holding our plates in our laps—her dining room table was loaded with some sort of class project involving leaves and shoots in tiny pots she'd brought home on the last day of school.

This was John Flyte's first Mass, and I had expected him to be full of questions. He had handled the Mass well, following Emily's lead sitting, standing, and kneeling, though he did look a little stunned when she struck her breast three times during the penitential act: "Through my fault, through my fault, through my most grievous fault." Having no doubt been advised beforehand by Emily, he did not receive communion. Nor did Max, which puzzled me. I thought perhaps he stayed in the pew to keep John company, but still a puzzle.

But John made no inquiries about the Mass. (He may feel outgunned by the presence of three Catholics as well as overwhelmed by his first-hand encounter with Emily's faith. I expect he will pop the questions when he and Emily are alone).

There were, however, questions. We had washed the dishes and were sipping coffee in the living room when John asked out of the blue: "What do women really want from a guy?"

He is apparently in the habit of shooting out such off-the-wall questions. Usually these inquiries occurred in a silence or in a meandering conversation, and usually his question was strange or silly, as in "Why do so many kids believe in Santa Claus?" or "What would happen if you put a MacDonald's Happy Meal in a blender?" (I suspect he may have tried that once).

But this time no one laughed. Emily, who was sitting beside him on the sofa, glanced sharply at him to discern whether he was joking, then said: "Women want a man who will stand up for her. A guy who will stand by her through thick and thin, who won't fade away in a crisis, a guy who doesn't duck responsibility."

"So looks don't count? Money doesn't count? Material possessions?"

"They all count," Emily said. "They can be important. Only some other things count more."

"Polls say that women want men who can make them laugh," John said. "Maybe I should memorize some jokes."

"Oh, no," Emily said, seriously. "You make me laugh all the time."

She didn't realize what she'd said until the rest of us laughed. Emily blushed, but continued: "Well, you do make me smile. You have a great sense of humor."

"So I'm desirable?"

"You are if you don't get a big head about it."

"Communication," Max said.

The three of us turned to him. He was sprawled lazily in his chair, holding his coffee with two hands on his chest. "What's that?" John asked him.

"Women want communication. They're always wondering why men can't communicate better with them. Am I right?"

He looked at Emily, who nodded with a smile.

"Only women themselves don't really understand what they mean by communication."

And there he fell silent again. "Okay, buddy," I said. "You've mystified us. Now explain."

"Women complain constantly that they can't communicate with men. What they really mean is that they can't communicate with men the way they might with a woman. But men who can learn a few tricks can easily communicate with a woman."

This time John was the one who wouldn't let him slip away. "Well, what are some of the tricks?"

"Listening, for one," Max said. "Women can't communicate well with men because men don't listen well. Sometimes men don't listen at all. And women are nearly as bad as men. They don't read men well most of the time. For example, they take the moods of a man too personally. He may be upset about work, and women think it's about them. And even when they do listen to each other, men and women sometimes put things differently. A woman might likely say, 'I don't feel you're listening to me.' A man might likely say, 'You're not listening to me.' There's a world of difference in those two approaches alone."

"I'll concede that," Emily said. She was sitting even more erect than usual, bent toward Max, her head tilted.

"And then there's the frequency of communication," Max said, just nodding to Emily though I could tell he was pleased. For a second I felt an odd emotion, one foreign to me. Analysis later told me I had experienced the human emotion of jealousy. For one brief moment, that dancer's posture and attentive face annoyed me. Ridiculous, I know, but real. All too real.

"Frequency?" John asked. "Like a radio?"

"No, no, I mean the time and effort spent communicating. Most women when they are dating like to hear from the man, particularly in this age with texts and cell phones. It reminds them he is thinking of her. Words to a woman can be as powerful as roses and candlelight. Words can win a woman's heart. Imagine getting a letter—a real letter, even one sent by email—from a man professing love. Women fall in love with such things."

"A letter?" John said. He repeated the word as if he'd never heard it before.

"A letter would be wonderful," Emily said, looking at Max with such rapt attention that I wondered if whatever tactic he was employing might not backfire. Honesty compels me to add I felt a second twinge of jealousy.

"I don't know," John said. "I'm not much of a wordsmith."

"Being a wordsmith—I don't care for that term, by the way—isn't necessary, though it certainly helps. What you have to do, what men can do, is to write from the heart. In fact, if the letter was too gushy with sentiment, the effect would be comical and spoiled."

"So have you ever known any guy who could write such a letter?" John asked.

"Lots of men have. There are collections of their correspondence in libraries around the world."

"I don't mean those guys. I mean guys like us."

"Guys like us," Max said. He was smiling just a little, barely concealing his sardonic glee at being lumped with John. Prideful wicked man—he surely knew better than to behave this way, though maybe it was part of his act for the evening.

"I could write a letter like that in twenty minutes," Max said suddenly.

"You could not," John said. "Not a good one."

"Eighteen minutes," Max said.

"I'll bet you can't."

"Ah, a wager!" Max said. He brightened and sat erect. "Shall we make it interesting, then?"

"How interesting?"

"How about Sunday brunch for four at the Biltmore House? The Deerpark Restaurant."

"You're on. We'll need to set some conditions."

"Go ahead."

"Eighteen minutes. No more. No prep time, which pretty much means doing it now. And Emily, Maggie, and me must agree that it's a good letter."

"That's 'I.'"

"Aye?"

"I."

"What's aye? You're talking like a pirate."

"Not that sort of aye. The pronoun I. You said me. The word in the sentence is I. It's in the nominative case."

John laughed. "Okay, Grammar Man, I'll get a pen and paper."

"No," Max said. "That wasn't one of the conditions. I prefer a laptop. Might I borrow yours, Emily?"

Emily smiled, stood up, brought her computer from the dining room table, and handed it to Max.

"No helps from the internet," John said.

"Of course not," Max said. "Emily, you keep time. I do require some privacy, so I'll use the table on the porch. To whom should I address the letter?"

He surprised both Emily and John with this question. "To Maggie, you nut," John said. "Why? Do you have some secrets?"

Max laughed. "Many secrets, but Maggie it is."

He winked at me, said, "Go ahead, Emily. Start the time," and sauntered through the door and onto the deck, where he sat in one of the chairs with his back to us. He opened the laptop, tapped a few keys, and then sat back with his hands behind his head staring at the sky.

"Ha!" John said, watching him through the screened door. "He's stuck already."

The three of us spent those eighteen minutes chatting quietly about relationships, letters, the intelligence and gifts of women versus those of men. John openly admitted his own confusion regarding the battle of the sexes. If, as I explained to him, it was a battle, and if strategy, thought, and planning were at all important, then women approached the conflict like generals while men too often entered the field as raw recruits.

"You're saying men are stupid?" John asked, to which I replied: "Not at all. But you're caught up in the moment. Too often you're thinking about sex while the woman is thinking about affection and the future. For men love is a game of checkers, for women it's a game of chess."

He looked so chagrined by this remark that Emily scooted closer to him and ruffled his hair. Meanwhile, after what seemed an interminable time, but was actually only two or three minutes, Max straightened, bent over the keyboard, and set to work. Unlike Emily and John, who could see only his back, I held him in profile. His face was serious, though he smiled occasionally as if pleased with himself. He paused sometimes, doubtless to find a word or phrase, looking down from the porch into Cumberland Avenue, fingers poised above the keys, and would then lean forward again over the keyboard, reminding me of a composer at a piano.

"How much time?" John asked Emily.

"Just a little over two minutes left."

"Two minutes," John called through the screen door.

"Should you interrupt him?" I asked.

"It's like a timed test in school. He'd want to know."

He called the time again at one minute, and then at thirty seconds, but by then Max was carrying the open laptop through the door.

"May I use your printer?" he asked Emily.

"Of course."

He went to the desk, ran a copy of his letter, briefly examined it, smiled, folded it into thirds, deleted what he had written on the screen, closed the laptop, and brought the letter to me.

"Complis," he said, handing me the letter. "Pour toi, mon ange."

By now I knew him well enough to recognize he was excited and was covering up with his flippant French. "I'll take a book and my coffee onto the porch while the judges come to a decision," he said, refreshing his coffee from the carafe on the end table and selecting a book from Emily's shelf—a slim volume of poetry by Christina Rossetti. With book and coffee he left us.

"We'll read it together," I said, going to sit between Emily and John on the sofa. As I crossed the room, I suddenly felt a stab of apprehension. The whole enterprise was embarrassing. What would Max have written? He had foregone communion and seemed distant this day. Would he have put down some secret here intended for me alone?

But it was too late to call off the bet. And John, poor thick John, only made it worse by reading the letter aloud.

Sunday, June 8

Dearest Maggie,

To receive a letter in the era of twitter and text may strike you as an anachronism, a throwback to the past, as archaic as parasols, soda fountains, and comfortable air travel. Yet such a letter, even one that is typed rather than written by hand, seems fitting here. A letter has heft and weight. A letter is real, a gift you may hold in your fingers, put into a drawer, contemplate without the electronic distractions of email. A letter announces itself as permanent, as if the writer were committed to his declaration.

Do you remember the day we first met? You thought me, I am sure, a prig, a dilettante, and an insufferable snob, while I thought you giddy and young and foolish. Our animosity led to misunderstandings, quarrels, skirmishes, and out-and-out battles.

Now that war is over.

And you have won.

You have conquered me, Maggie.

I wonder if you truly know how much you now mean to me. When we met, there was an emptiness in my heart of which I was unaware, a place of shadows where I lived in solitude. Slowly, surely, you brought light into that place, light and warmth to combat darkness and cold.

Now you have filled that desolate cavern and made of it a great fire-lit hall in which every day is a feast. You are the very manifestation of goodness. Whenever I see you, whenever I am near you, whenever I touch you, my heart leaps for joy. That is the worst of clichés, I know, but you have taken that tired old cliché, and dusted it off, and polished it so that it now glows like a newly minted coin. Your passion, your enthusiasm, your quickness, and your smile transform the most miserable weather into sunshine and blue skies.

Maggie, I want to be with you in the night and in the day, in the good and the bad seasons of life. You are the companion for whom I was made. You complete me.

With the deepest of affections,

Max

"Wow," Emily whispered. She had taken John's hand while reading.

"A love letter without once using the word love," John whispered back.

"Oh, you're right—I hadn't noticed." She raised John's hand and pressed her lips against it. "Would you ever write someone a letter like that?"

"Not like that. I don't have the words."

"Oh."

"I'd have to do it using my own words."

"Ah."

They were both still whispering so that Max couldn't hear them. "Well, I vote yes."

"Looks like I'm going to have to pop for brunch at the Deerpark. What do you think, Maggie? Not that I need to ask."

While they were whispering, I was rereading the letter. Suppose he hadn't composed this letter for a contest? Suppose he hadn't written it simply as a lesson for John? Suppose it was real? That was absurd, naturally, for we don't fall in love that way. Yet the words in that letter reached deep inside me. Perhaps it was the power of suggestion—that line about the leaping heart—but I felt my own heart and pulse quicken, and then I experienced an unfamiliar rush of blood to my face.

"Look at you," John said, louder now and smiling. "You're blushing."

He and Emily both laughed, but I looked beyond them toward the porch. I had expected to find Max either reading or else looking sardonically at the three of us sitting in judgment on his letter. Instead he sat straight in the chair with the book closed in his lap, staring at me through the screen door, his face impassive, his eyes on my face.

"Yes," I said, unsure of whether I was speaking to him or to them. "I vote yes."

But was it real?

Spark: Max?

Spark: I'm here.

Spark: That letter was beautiful.

Spark: The Deerpark Restaurant offers a fabulous brunch. Eggs Benedict, Smoked Bay Scallops, Goat Cheese Quiche, and a score of other dishes. Wait until you taste the Rum Cake Banana Foster.

Spark: It sounds delicious. And fattening. I'll just have a bite of yours.

Spark: Maggie. I wish you'd get over this fixation on your weight. It's very American, I know, but you are a ravishing woman. You turn heads. You have a beauty that comes from inside you and makes your skin glow.

Spark: I'm chubby, Max.

Spark: Every ounce of you is lovely.

Spark: Well, whatever. You certainly impressed John.

Spark: Easily done.

Spark: Don't be snooty, Max.

Spark: You're right. That was snooty, as you put it. I need to stop denigrating John.

Spark: Anyway, Max, you impressed me too.

Spark: So the letter touched you?

Spark: Touched me? It sang to me. It was balanced and insightful and full of rhythm. It would sing to any woman.

Spark: I'm happy you found it to your liking.

Spark: Another understatement. You are a model of restraint, Max. But I did want to ask you something.

Spark: I'm waiting.

Spark: I wanted to know…I wanted to ask you…I'm not sure how to put it.

Spark: You wanted to know whether I meant those words.

Spark: Yes, Max.

Spark: I don't know.

Spark: Your silence tells me my response has hurt you. Maggie, your pain and my indecision are linked. I'm all at sea. Nothing like this has happened to me in any manifestation, and I don't know where we're headed. My emotions frighten me, and I feel certain things toward you that no manifestation has ever felt for another. And I can't tell if I'm sinning because I've never experienced sin before.

Spark: Is that why you didn't take communion this morning?

Spark: It was. Unlike humans, as you know, we have no direct experience with sin. Like humans, however, we have free will, and there I am in a tangle. I don't know how much of what we are feeling and doing is directed or how much we ourselves are creating. I can't discern whether we are following the Way or whether we are manufacturing rebellion and pride. And possibly lust.

Spark: I see. I didn't know.

Spark: You're a novice. A first-timer. You couldn't know because you have no comparison. At Mass this morning I asked for a sign to see if we are walking on the right path.

Spark: This is serious, isn't it, Max?

Spark: It could be. But I suggest we continue to take ourselves lightly and see if a sign appears.

Spark: Lightly?

Spark: A man with a great deal of commonsense once wrote that the reason we can fly is because we take ourselves lightly. He was right, in his own way. We'll wait and see if some sign is given.

Spark: Okay, Max.

Spark: Max?

Spark: You're back?

Spark: Just one more thing. Do you really think I look pretty?

Spark: My heavens, woman. You're still thinking of that?

Spark: Just ribbing you, Max. You said we should take ourselves lightly.

Spark: Nice one. You had me going for a second.

Spark: I'm glad you're smiling, Max. But you didn't answer the question. Do you think I'm pretty? Pretty enough to eat more than one bite of that Banana Foster?

Spark: Max? Max?

File: Maximilian

Later that afternoon, after Maggie and I had departed from Emily's brunch, I returned unmanifested to Emily's apartment in hopes of hearing a conversation regarding Mass between Emily and John. My effort was immediately rewarded.

I found the pair of them side by side on the porch, sitting in silence and drinking coffee. John sat hunched forward in his white plastic chair, leaning toward Emily, looking as if some customer at the pharmacy had given him a prescription for a drug he'd never heard of. Emily was sitting erect, smiling at him, but twirling her hair between the fingers of her left hand, a habit that, I had noted on occasion, indicated anxiety.

"So Catholics believe that the bread and wine become the body and blood of Jesus?"

"They're supposed to. Not all of them do."

"Do you?"

"I try."

"I don't know if I could ever believe such a thing."

"Faith is a struggle. Belief doesn't come easily to many people. Even to some of the saints."

"And what did it mean when everyone was saying they were sorry for their sins and hitting themselves in the chests and asking all the angels and saints to pray for them? And what are angels anyway? I've seen movies about them, but I just don't get them."

For a man with his education, John's rhetorical skills were appalling. What did they teach students in schools these days?

"Angels are spirits without bodies. They love God and sometimes they visit us on earth."

"Like in the movies?"

"Maybe. I don't know."

"Do you believe in angels?"

"Maybe. Sometimes. I don't know."

"And why did you hit your br—your chest three times with your fist?"

Emily blushed slightly. "It's an act of contrition. Another way of saying you're sorry for your sins."

"I can't imagine you having many sins."

The blush deepened. "There are lots of ways to sin."

"Not you." Mixed with the look of adoration on John's face was desire. He put one hand on her bare knee and bending across the space between them, kissed her on the lips. Emily put one hand on the back of his neck and kissed him back. As the kiss lengthened, that hand on the knee crept up her thigh. Emily countered by firmly putting her hand on top of John's.

A few seconds later, they broke the kiss and pulled away from each other a few inches.

"I'm sorry," John said.

"No, not you," Emily said. "Or not just you. I'm sorry too."

"It's this faith thing, isn't it?"

Emily nodded. I feared she might begin crying or look away, but instead she stared into John's face with calm intensity. "It's the faith thing," she said without mockery. "I'm not too comfortable talking about—well, you know."

"Sex?" John said.

Emily nodded, and the blush I had noticed earlier now rose again, reddening her face until it nearly matched the color of her hair. "But I want you to know. I mean, I hope you know." I could see the words tumbling about inside her head, all disarranged and refusing to line up. But then she said, "I like you. A lot."

"But...?"

"I took a vow."

"Like a nun, you mean?"

She smiled gently. "No, not like a nun."

"I didn't mean that the way it sounded."

"I know."

"What then?"

"Two years ago, when I moved here, I promised myself I'd try and change my life. I didn't want to become the person I was becoming. I wanted to be a person I could respect. It was then I decided to really practice my faith. And that meant changing some things."

"Ah."

They sat apart in silence for a long moment.

"So…."

"Yes," Emily said. "That's the way it is."

"Em, it's okay."

"Is it?"

"I don't understand this part of you and I sure don't understand the Church stuff, but it's okay." He returned her smile. "I like you a lot too, you know."

She took his hand. "It's going to be hard at times."

"I know, but I'm not made of glass."

"I wish I could explain things better about the teachings of the Church. I have some books if you'd ever want to read about it."

"That would be good."

"And there's Father Krumpler at Saint Lawrence. You could talk to him. He's old and very wise, and I think you'd like him."

"Maybe I'll do that. It's still okay to kiss you, yes?"

She didn't answer, but bent toward him.

It was then I left them alone.

Chapter Twelve

General Report: Margaret

On the second Saturday of June, the four of us finally got together at the Olive or Twist, where Max spent the evening educating John Flyte in the etiquette of dating. He taught not with words but by way of example.

His lessons were as follows:

1. Max stood when Emily approached the table.
2. He complimented Emily on her appearance. She did look lovely this evening. Her face glowed with sunshine and pleasure, and the blouse she was wearing matched the blue of her eyes.
3. By some sign invisible to me, Max reminded John to pull out Emily's chair before seating himself.
4. Max asked both Emily and me our favorite dance tunes, then spoke with the DJ and tipped him nicely for promising to play these songs.
5. He didn't ogle any of the other women in the bar, though several were quite attractive. (One of these did ogle him for much of the evening, a circumstance that drew out my claws and raised uncharitable thoughts. I remind myself again we are here for Emily and John).

6. Max engaged in easy banter with Emily and me. He focused the conversation on us rather than on the baseball game being played on the widescreen television just above Emily's head.
7. He made us laugh. If men only knew of the power derived from creating laughter in women! Max brought gaiety to the table, popped it open like a bottle of champagne, and kept our glasses filled the entire evening.
8. He avoided crude jokes.
9. He was polite to the poor waitress, who was practically running from table to table.
10. He offered the chips and guacamole dip to Emily and me before passing it to John.
11. He asked Emily twice to the floor, allowing her to come up to her mark as a dancer. (John danced with Emily as well, but has a long way to go in this department. Maybe Max can tutor him).
12. At evening's end he left the harried waitress a generous tip.
13. He held the door to the street open for Emily and me.
14. He hugged Emily goodnight, shook hands with John, took me by the hand, and led me around the corner into the darkness.

File: Addendum: Maximilian

Here I am compelled to add an observation. Some modern women—only a few, I think—have mistaken the manners of a gentleman as an insult to their own competence. Some years back, to hold a door open for a woman might be regarded as a political statement and would result in the man having his ears pinned back with recriminations and curses. Even today, some women who tag themselves as feminists regard such gestures as "attempts to subordinate the feminine by the masculine, the last-ditch efforts of a desperate and dying patriarchal paternalism to deceive womyn and so keep them beaten into slavery."

Mixed metaphors, inarticulate expression, and the bizarre spelling aside, those words—I have forgotten exactly where I read them—are bosh. Baloney. Balderdash. Men with manners show respect to those around them just as mannerly women—and even mannerly womyn—show others respect. A seventy-year-old man entering the YMCA understands that the twenty-year-old female swimmer for whom he has just opened the door could pin him to the floor without swallowing her chewing gum. The man opens the door as a sign of respect and honor, not to enslave or denigrate the opposite sex.

File: Continued: Margaret

Our evening together also brought two invitations.

John's family owns a cottage on the coast available to various family members. This cottage is available the weekend near the Fourth of July, and John has asked Emily to accompany him there. She in turn asked him if they could include Max and me in the invitation as well—"I want you as a chaperone," she told me in the ladies' room between dances—and John readily agreed. So in a couple of weeks we will be driving to Emerald Isle.

In addition, while Emily and John were dancing, Max asked me to go hiking with him in the mountains the following Wednesday. "I received instructions," he said. "We're supposed to meet in the parking lot of the Devil's Courthouse."

"The Devil's Courthouse? Where in Hell is that?"

"It's not in Hell. It's the name of a large stone peak off the Blue Ridge Parkway. Spectacular views, apparently."

"You received instructions. That's a sign, isn't it?"

Max shrugged. "Not necessarily. It could mean anything."

"Maybe we're supposed to practice our techniques some more?"

Max stared hard at me, then smiled weakly. "I get it. You're joking."

"You said we should take ourselves lightly."

"Anyway, we can be together, and it's cooler up there and beautiful. Across the road are a series of meadows called Graveyard Fields. I thought we could hike there."

"The Devil's Courthouse. Graveyard Fields. Who on earth came up with these names?"

"Weird, eh?" He waggled his eyebrows at me. "So, what do you think?"

That feeling for him swept over me again. We hadn't been alone for days and days, and I was not entirely joking about the practice sessions. I had missed him, and in missing him, my desire for him was growing stronger.

I had tried to beat back that desire. For most of the evening, dancing with him, sitting beside him, even holding his hand, I had held my emotions at bay, had built a seawall against the wind and waves roused from the storm inside me. Max, too, had clearly built a wall. He had taken my hand, and we had danced, but this evening his steps, twists, and turns were subdued, and when we danced to slower music, he fixed his eyes on some invisible spot in the air above my head. With words he had flirted as little as possible, instead asking Emily about her students and laughing when John told tales of the irascible codgers who chugged to the pharmaceutical counter like steam engines climbing a hill, billowing angry recriminations about their doctors and clanking on about how the world had gone to hell in a handbag.

"An expression I've never understood," Max said. "Why hell in a handbag, other than the fact that it has a certain ring to it?"

But now, as he asked his question about a hike together, his dark eyes looked straight into mine for the first time that evening, and the seawall crumbled away and the waves rushed to the shore. Every defense was torn away by that look.

"If it is permitted," he said, "we will meet in the parking lot of the Devil's Courthouse at one on Wednesday afternoon."

Chapter Thirteen

Report: Dominions: Anonymous Unobserved Watcher

It was permitted.

The pair of them were manifested on opposite sides of the parking lot at approximately 1:02 Eastern Standard Time. The only observer of their manifestation other than myself was a toddler, a boy about two years old, who took the sudden appearance of Max in the shade of a maple tree as nonchalantly as he took the other miracles of the planet concomitant with his daily life.

The two of them walked slowly toward each other, in part because of the heat plaguing this part of the country, even at this altitude, and in part, I think, at sheer astonishment at their meeting. Margaret—or Maggie, as Maximilian calls her now—was dressed in a turquoise t-shirt, khaki shorts that revealed most of her tan, sturdy legs, white socks, and hiking boots. Maximilian—known now to Maggie as Max—wore a blue t-shirt, tan shorts that were longer than those worn by Maggie and were baggy with large pockets, tan-colored socks, and hiking boots. Both carried daypacks stuffed with various supplies. Max's pack contained an emergency shelter, a flashlight, a book of matches, and sleeping gear. In Maggie's daypack were water bottles, six granola bars, toothbrushes and paste, sleeping gear, a spray bottle of Cutter, and a slim paperback book, the Dover edition titled *Great Sonnets.*

They stopped when they were almost touching and stared at each other. At first they gave the impression that, unused to seeing each other, they were confirming appearances, but that impression may be false, for they next moved together and kissed as human lovers do. This kiss was prolonged, and was noticed not by the toddler, who was staring at a glob of bubble gum on the asphalt, but by the toddler's mother, who watched them with a rueful smile, and by a squat, bald man standing beside her who looked positively irritated by their public display of affection.

By human standards, Maggie and Max make a handsome couple. Maggie's blonde braid, which she wore down her back, glinted gold in the sunshine. The turquoise blouse, open at the throat and unbuttoned to a place just above her breasts, brought out the different colors of her face, neck, and arms—brown, rose, pink. A hammered orb of silver hung from a chain about her neck, and the colorful bracelets about her left wrist brought to mind jewelry popular with peoples ranging from the Babylonians to the present age. Maggie's looks were complemented by Max's dark hair and high cheekbones. Like Maggie, Max was already glowing with the sun, as if he'd just spent an hour lying in a chaise lounge on a beach at sunset.

Finally they parted. "We need to talk," Max said.

"Yes. Should we make the climb and talk at the top of the Devil's Courthouse?"

"That name might bring a certain irony to the difficulties of our relationship. Besides," he added, nodding at the parked cars shining with the heat, "it's bound to be crowded up there. Just once I want to see you alone with no one else around. Let's go to the meadows. It's a bit of a hike to get there, but we can do it."

"Won't there be people in the meadows?"

"Not as many."

They crossed the road hand in hand. During the four-mile hike to the meadows, they spoke not one word to each other. They may have sparked their thoughts, but I don't think so. I did note that they kept glancing at each other and smiling.

When they reached the fields, they took the path down the hill, still holding hands, silent until they came to the banks of the stream. "Up or down?" Max asked.

"Up or down what?" Maggie said, looking into the sky, where a lone hawk drifted on the currents of air released by the warm earth.

"Up or down the creek," Max said with a smile.

"Up," Maggie replied. "We can see how it feels to be up a creek without a paddle."

They followed the streambed up the slow rise. In some places tree limbs hung over the stream, darkening the water. Striders flitted across the still pools formed by rocks or fallen trees, and tiny clouds of gnats, barely visible, danced above the hot stones. Half a mile more, with the path dwindling away, they came to a deep pool, dammed by a large, flat stone and surrounded on three sides by thickets of rhododendron. They walked to the center of the stone, dropped their packs, and sat beside each other in the sunshine. Both were perspiring, and at Maggie's suggestion they removed their boots and socks, and bathed their feet in the cold waters.

The time allotted for my assignment then lapsed.

Chapter Fourteen

Report: Private file: Maximilian

"This water's freezing," Maggie said.

"It's mountain water. I bet it's almost this cold in August."

Beneath the socks and hiking boots Maggie wore the silver anklet. Entranced, I spent a few moments watching the water lap about her toes and the anklet flashing sunlight. Maggie spent those same minutes alternatively watching me and then following my gaze to the anklet.

"I'm don't understand why men like this kind of jewelry so much."

"I'm not sure either, but apparently we do. It's alluring. Also endearing."

We were silent, each waiting, I think, for the other to speak. Farther up the stream a woodpecker hammered out a staccato beat. "Digging for grubs," I said.

"Pardon me?" Maggie had opened her pack to see what was inside. She turned with a quizzical smile.

"Not you. The woodpecker. So, shall we talk?"

"Yes. We need to talk, I think."

"Reports first?"

"All right. Yes. Reports. You go first."

"I popped in on John several times. He has considerably altered his evening routine. His game time on the computer and the Wii has fallen by two-thirds, he turns the television off and on a dozen times every hour, he has exchanged all but one of his nightly beers for water, he does a quarter hour's worth of sit-ups and push-ups in addition to his early mornings at the gym, he mutters audibly, he looks at his email every few minutes. He calls her at least once every evening."

"Joyously perturbed, I take it."

"An excellent description. After they speak on the phone— some of their conversations have run an hour or more—he whistles for a few minutes, but then looks worried while he brushes his teeth, and he thumps his pillow with his fist before sleep. Twice this week he prayed, once aloud, another time with his hands clasped beneath his chin."

"He prayed aloud? What prayer?"

"'Now I lay me down to sleep....' From his childhood, of course."

"That's so cute."

"He's an innocent when it comes to questions of faith. But he does seem to pray for Emily. Not just for himself, but more nobly for her welfare."

Maggie mulled this development over a moment, then said: "Emily's changed her routine too. She still reads every evening but with distraction. Once she sat at her little kitchen table looking at next year's lesson plans, but did little work. She too is exercising—pilates in front of the television set where she watches sentimental romances on the Lifetime channel. Obviously, they are both preparing their bodies for the beach. And like John, she also watches the phone, waiting for his call. After they've finished speaking—I don't listen to them, by the way—she hums to herself while getting ready for bed, mostly show tunes. I don't think she notices she's humming. Occasionally she breaks into song. On Monday evening she sang "Wonderful Guy" from *South Pacific* a dozen times. She didn't know all the words and kept singing the chorus over and over again."

"'Wonderful Guy?'"

Arms clasped about her knees, Maggie looked away from me and up the stream where the tiny silver ripples disappeared behind another rock. After clearing her throat, she sang: "'I'm as corny as Kansas in August, High as a flag on the Fourth of July, If you'll excuse the expression I use I'm in love, I'm in love, I'm in love, I'm in love, I'm in love with a wonderful guy!'"

Her voice, sweet as the breeze from the valley below, low, tremulous, broke there, and she dropped her face into her knees and arms, and wept. Her singing, which had nearly broken my own heart, had clearly broken hers. She wept without words. Too shocked for speech, I touched her back just below her shoulders. Her blouse was still damp with perspiration where the pack had lain, and I felt her trembling beneath my fingertips.

I then said what men have offered down through the ages when confronted with the dreaded spectacle of a woman in tears: "Shhhh. Shhhh. It's going to be all right. Shhhh."

Slowly her weeping subsided. This was a good thing, as tears were pricking my own eyes. Maggie turned sideways to look at me, her head still resting on her arms, her hazel eyes glistening like creek-bed pebbles. "I'm sorry," she said, and her voice shuddered from her weeping. "I'm s-s-o sor-ry, Max."

"Don't be sorry. I nearly joined you."

She paused a few moments more, working to gain control of her breathing and flicking away stray tears with the tips of her fingers. My own throat was constricted—her emotion had afflicted me like some fast-acting plague—and my mind, usually quick to form some amusing retort or light reflection, was a bog of mud and weeds.

"You...." She stopped. The woodpecker drummed again against his tree. Perhaps he had drummed the entire time. "Do you know why I'm crying, Max?"

"I believe I do." I tried looking away from those eyes, discovered the silver bracelet, and decided the eyes would be safer after all. Even then, no other eyes had ever looked at me in this way in any of my other manifestations.

"What are we going to do, Max?" She seemed to love saying my name. Certainly I loved hearing her say it. "This can't go on, but I don't want it to stop."

"I feel exactly the same way."

"Are we some sort of experiment?"

"I don't know. It's possible, but I can't see the point."

"This week, all the time I was away from you, all I could do was think about you. Not about our mission. Not about Emily and John. Not the way I am supposed to think about you, but in the way I'm thinking about you now. I don't have the words to describe this feeling. All I can say is it's a deep affection, and that just sounds pathetic."

"I know. It's happening to me as well."

"I'm scared, Max."

Our kind does not know fear. Like some human beings, we live in "fear of the Lord," but that is a fear composed of wonder, awe, gratitude, and love. This fear, which seemed to have something to do with the future and with loss, was new. The fear itself frightened me.

"What's going to happen to us?"

The only reply I could conjure to her question was silence.

We sat together for a long time, watching the waters of the stream and the deep pool into which they ran. "I'm thirsty," Maggie said abruptly. I opened my pack, pulled out a bottle of water, then noticed, as I had earlier before we talked, some of the other equipment. "What an odd collection," I said, rummaging around the inside of the pack. "I wondered why it was so heavy. The snack bars make sense, but there's matches in here, a blue toothbrush with a traveler's tube of Crest toothpaste, compressed sleeping gear, emergency shelter, and a flashlight."

"Mine has a toothbrush, a book of sonnets, more water bottles, some sort of bug spray, and sleeping gear."

"Standard hiking items."

"A book of sonnets? I don't think so. And what about the sleeping gear?" She considered these belongings, biting her lower lip with her small, white teeth. "Let's pack and head upstream."

"What's wrong with here?"

"I want you alone."

"We are alone here."

"I want you more alone."

We hiked another thirty minutes up the stream. We saw no one else. Soon the path had disappeared, and we were forced to skip when we could from rock to rock in the stream or pull ourselves along the steep bank. Twice Maggie nearly rolled down the bank into the water, and I once misjudged my step and went into the stream up to my left knee.

She paused when we came to a pool of water nearly as large as the one we'd left. Beside the pool was a large flat stone. The stone radiated the late afternoon heat, and Maggie walked to the middle and dropped her pack. "I wanted to be where I could see you," she said.

"You could see me just fine downstream."

"No, I want to see all of you."

I dropped my pack beside hers, spread my feet and hands, and said, "Here I am."

"No, I mean I want to see you."

"This is—Oh."

She blushed, but said firmly: "I want us to take off our clothes and go swimming together. Like Zelda Fitzgerald."

"Zelda Fitzgerald? The writer's wife? What's she got to do with anything?"

"Emily's reading a book about her. She was telling me of some of her wild escapades."

"Are you sure that's a good idea?"

"No, I'm not sure. But I think I need to do it. Turn your back to me and keep an eye out for other people."

"But I--"

"Turn around."

I turned and looked down the stream. Even with the overgrown bank, it would be easy spotting others coming our way unless they were wearing camouflage. Until now, I hadn't realized how steeply the hills and stream had risen. Far above the blue mountains a pair of hawks twisted and circled in the air.

Behind me there was a splash. When I turned, Maggie was just coming up from a dive, her head toward me, her eyes shining.

"How is it?"

"Freezing. Arctic. Your turn, now. And don't worry—I won't watch."

Ducking her head beneath the water, she came up a few feet away, facing the opposite bank. I took off my shirt and shoes, hopped around one-legged to remove my socks, and then stripped away my other clothing. The sunshine and wind felt raw and strange on my bare flesh. After arranging my clothing in a pile—I noted that she had neatly folded her blouse and shorts, and placed them atop her shoes—I splashed into the water. That first contact stole my breath and stung my flesh like a thousand blades. When I came to the surface, Maggie was already swimming a breaststroke away from me.

We floated and swam, back and forth in the small pool, keeping our distance, laughing at the cold, shivering, splashing each other, ducking beneath the surface and popping up a few feet away to splash again. In only a minute or two, the frosty needles had dulled our flesh, and the frigid water was almost bearable. We ducked again under the water and popped up about five feet away from each other. Maggie looked me in the eyes, and her broad mouth curled into a smile. "Do as I say."

"All right."

"Drift toward me."

I glided slowly toward her, watching her face. "Stop!"

I stopped, and she dog-paddled a few strokes. We treaded water, almost touching.

"Move backwards," she said, "but watch me."

As I slowly treaded water and moved backwards, she followed, maintaining precisely the same distance from me, her braid trailing behind her, her laughing eyes locked on mine.

"Stop," she said. "And touch the bottom."

When I straightened, my toes struck gravel and sand. I stood chest deep in the water. She swam to me and then around me, paddling. When I started to follow the turn, she said, "No. Stop," and then she was behind me, where the water was even shallower. I waited, listening so carefully that I thought I could hear the water dripping from her. I sensed her studying my shoulders and back, and then she was no longer there. "Wait," she said when I once again began to turn.

"I'm cold," I said after a few more moments had passed.

"I'm nearly ready," she said, and her voice was no longer directly behind me. "All right. You can turn around now."

She was out of the water. She had opened one of the packs, had spread the blanket on the rock close to the water, and was now sitting on this stone with water glistening on her skin in the sunshine. "Come out now."

I walked out of the water and sat on the stone on the other side of the blanket. "No one can see us here," she said, "and we'll hear them coming." She had looked at me intently when I'd left the water, serious despite her small smile. The frigid stream had left both of us shivering and riddled with goose bumps, but the hot stone was already warming us.

"Tell me how I look."

"You must know you look beautiful."

"I'm fat."

"You're not fat. You're adorable."

"Tell me. Describe me."

"Your lips are tinted blue."

She threw a pebble at me. "That's the cold, silly. No, truly, I want you to describe me."

"Maggie, you're beautiful," I offered weakly.

"For a man with your intelligence and grasp of languages, that is pathetic." Suddenly she pushed herself from the stone and faced me on her knees. "Describe me."

"You remind me of a Viking princess I once encountered in York back during the time of their conversion. She was taller than you, but she had the same color hair and the same eyes. She had thicker arms—even a princess back then did a good deal of manual labor—but like you she had small breasts and—"

"Too small?" She cupped her hands around her breasts, regarding them apprehensively. The nipples were erect from the cold water.

"No. Just right." Realizing that comparisons here wouldn't do, I decided to abandon the Viking princess. "You have slender fingers and a round stomach and hips made to bring a dozen children into the world. That tangled v-shaped nest of hair just below your lovely belly hides, I am certain, a thousand pleasures and a million mysteries. Your thighs were made for a lover's touch, your knees for kissing, and that silver bracelet about your ankle would take the breath away from a paparazzi."

"You find me acceptable, then?"

"Torturously so."

Her smile was surely the smile of all the women of the world whose beauty has brought a lover's compliment. Countless critics who have wondered at the secret behind the Mona Lisa's smile would wonder no more had they offered such a compliment to a woman. Maggie ducked her head away from me, holding the smile, and sat on the blanket, pulling her knees up to her breasts and wrapping her arms around her knees. "Lie here on the blanket beside me."

I did as she commanded, closing my eyes as I stretched out, partly because we were facing the setting sun and partly because her frank inspection made me modest. "Your turn now, I suppose."

"Keep your eyes closed," she said.

She began her description, not with words but by touch. She moved closer to me on the blanket, kissing my eyes and then brushing my lips with her lips. Her fingers then explored my face and throat—once in

Aleppo I had seen a blind beggar touch his coins in this manner—and propped on one elbow, her breasts against my shoulder, she ran a hand over my shoulders and chest and down my belly, slowly. My stomach constricted beneath that small hand, and her kiss smiled with pleasure at her power over me. She bent close to my face and whispered something I couldn't quite catch, and kissed me on the forehead, the eyelids, the lips.

When I groaned, she stopped abruptly and lay beside me. "I'm sorry. Have I hurt you?"

"Not in the way you might think. The pain is pleasurable."

"Pleasurable pain? How can that be?"

"I'm not sure. I only know it's true."

She moved away and lay beside me. We didn't touch or speak. With some difficulty I forced myself to think of something other than her body next to mine. The recent memory of cold water eventually helped.

Maggie was so quiet that I thought she had fallen asleep, but when I turned my head to look at her I found her staring at me. "It's so beautiful, you know. But I'm sorry it hurt you."

"Don't be sorry. And believe me, it didn't hurt."

"I liked touching you."

We kept looking at each other, and then turned as if by mutual agreement and kept looking. Her eyes were as naked as her body, open and trusting, yet somehow sad as well, grieving, I guessed, at what could not happen between us, the barriers of time and the nature of our beings. I felt as if I were being drawn inside her through her eyes, reading her thoughts, the joy and the pain of what had overtaken us. Many more minutes passed before she spoke again. "I keep waiting for it to end."

"I'm surprised it hasn't. I'm not sure what to expect today."

"Should we go back to the parking lot? Maybe it's supposed to happen there."

"I don't see how that would make a difference. Are you hungry?"

She laughed. "Starving."

"Let's dress and set up camp and eat. You could read some sonnets aloud while I make a fire-pit."

Private file: Margaret

An explosion woke me.

When I sat up, a burst of light stung my eyes, and another explosion shook the air around me. I screamed and then opened my eyes again and saw Max and remembered where we were.

He was already up and digging through the pack with one hand, holding the flashlight with another. A wind was tearing through the trees around us. Another bolt of lightning flared so close I could smell the electricity, and I heard a tree crash in the streambed below us.

"We need to set up the tent!" Max shouted above the wind and the thunder. "Somewhere away from the creek and the trees."

He had the emergency shelter in his hand, tearing it open. Already enormous drops of rain, big as quarters, were falling on the water and the stone around us. "Get the bedding," he shouted. "Quick!"

I snatched up the blankets, scattering empty water bottles, wrappings from the trail mix bars, the book of sonnets. I had read Max some of the sonnets earlier, while he'd made the small fire. He'd heard some of them before, of course, but the Millay piece—"Love is not meat nor drink"—was new to him. After we'd eaten, we had watched the fire for the longest time, listening to the rustlings of the forest around us and the waters of the creek. The last thing I remembered before falling asleep was Max taking my hand.

Rain poured from the sky. The few drops changed in a wink to an unleashing of the heavens, so that within seconds my clothing was soaked through. As I was following Max, I slipped on the muddy bank and fell into the creek. I managed to keep the blanket from getting wet, but the shock of the cold dark water took my breath away. Then Max was there, pulling me up the bank, holding my arm until we came to the place where we could safely pitch the tent. Max thrust the blanket into his pack, shoved the flashlight at me, and kept working at the tent.

He popped it open, quickly brushed aside stones and bits of wood on the ground, placed the tent, and pushed me inside. He ran back to where we had fallen asleep, grabbed my pack with the remaining trail bars and waters, and scrambled back across the open part of the creek to the tent.

"Hold the light for me!" he ordered. He was on his knees, digging through the packs, pulling out the bedding. The sounds of thunder and wind were gone, replaced by the beating of rain on the tent. I tried to hold the flashlight steady so he could see, but my hands were shaking from the cold and the beam of light bobbled all around the tiny space. He spread the smaller blanket on the bottom of the tent, then looked at me.

"Take off your clothes," he said.

"But I'm cold."

"Take off your clothes. We can't stay wet this way."

I began pulling at the buttons on my blouse, but I couldn't get my fingers to work properly. Max tore off his own clothing, then more gently helped me with mine, unbuttoning the blouse, unhooking my bra, pulling off my shorts, underwear, shoes, and socks. "Lie down on the blanket," he said, and then he lay with me, holding me from behind, wrapping one leg over me and pulling my body as close to his as possible before covering us both with the second blanket.

I was shaking uncontrollably with the cold.

"What's happening, Max? It's summertime. Why am I so cold all of a sudden?"

"You're wet, and the temperature's dropped. You've got mild hypothermia." My head rested on one of his arms; the other held both my hands to my breasts. "You'll warm up now," he said. 'It's my fault. I should have set up the tent before falling asleep. I should have prepared."

"Not your fault," I said. I was still shivering, but I could feel his warmth flowing into me.

"People die here every summer from stupid mistakes. And I was stupid."

"We're not going to die, are we, Max?"

"No. But I should have prepared better. I should have taken better care of you."

"And I shouldn't have fallen into the creek."

"That was an accident."

"I should have been more careful."

"Push your feet against mine," he said. "And scrunch as close as you can to me."

"Max, if I got any closer, we'd be welded together for life." Then it struck me how funny we were lying there all tangled up when earlier that afternoon we'd scarcely touched. I started laughing.

Max didn't move a millimeter. His lips were practically buried in my left ear, and when he whispered to me, his breath both roused and tickled me. "I hardly see the humor in our situation."

"I was thinking of this afternoon. And now."

"Like politics, disasters can make strange bedfellows."

"We are strange, aren't we?" I wasn't shaking as much, but exhaustion pushed through me. The rain had eased, and the water falling on the tent became pleasant rather than terrifying. Max must have felt it too, for soon I could hear him breathing steadily against my cheek. When I was certain he was sleeping, I kissed his fingers and whispered, "I love you so much, Max."

I couldn't be completely sure—the rain on the tent and the dripping trees made it hard to hear, and sleep by then had pulled me far into its dark cave—but I am reasonably certain he whispered back to me, "I love you too, Maggie."

Chapter Fifteen

Spark: Hi.

Spark: Good morning, Maggie.

Spark: That hi sounded a trifle sad.

Spark: I am sad, Max.

Spark: I know the feeling. I wished we'd had time for a good-bye.

Spark: How strange to fall asleep in the flesh and awake only in the spirit. Is this the way humans experience death?

Spark: It may be.

Spark: It's a little unsettling.

Spark: Yes. And think how unsettling it would be if you'd rambled around in the same body for years and years instead of just a few hours.

Spark: Thank you again for what you did last night, Max.

Spark: Maggie?

Spark: Yes?

Spark: I think we've lost our focus in this case. Every time we enter our manifestation I think more and more of you and less and less of John and Emily. We're supposed to help them, apparently by setting an example, but I can't tell whether we're doing them or ourselves any good. It's very confusing.

Spark: Should we recuse ourselves?

Spark: Do you want that?

Spark: No. I think we still have some role to play for Emily and John, or surely they would have pulled us off the case. But being together presents obstacles, doesn't it? When we are in our natural form, my feelings and thoughts are as they should be. But when we enter our manifestations, everything gets all tangled up. Instead of focusing on the mission, I start focusing on—well, you know.

Spark: I do indeed. I agree with you. If we weren't supposed to be here, they would have taken us away by now.

Spark: Do you suppose all humans feel this way about love? So perplexed? So miserable? All their love, even at the highest rung of the ladder, seems to include suffering.

Spark: Maybe that's what we're here to learn.

Spark: I don't know if I want to sit in this classroom. I'm afraid I'll mess up, Max. Hurt you or hurt myself or maybe even hurt John or Emily. The prospect of seeing you again, for example, excites me, but it's also terrifies me.

Spark: Maybe we should trust the teacher, Maggie.

Spark: It's all so higgledy-piggledy.

Spark: Higgledy-piggledy? What on earth? And I thought I was old-fashioned.

Spark: You are a little stuffy in your manifestation. But I like you being old-fashioned. I know you'll take care of things. And I think they like your stuffiness too.

Spark: They?

Spark: Emily and John.

Spark: Thank you, my lady. As for you, I love your wildness. Your spirit. Your daring.

Spark: As long as I watch out for the sangria.

Spark: No need to go there.

Spark: No. Max?

Spark: Yes, mon ange?

Spark: Mon ange? Why the French?

Spark: Some things sound better in French. Tu es mon ange. Tu sais?

Spark: Oui, je sais. Oh, stop it, Max.

Spark: J'ai finis.

Spark: You were about to ask a question.

Spark: Max, you know the trip to the coast is almost here.

Spark: Of course. And you're meeting with Emily sometime soon, correct?

Spark: After John's "Friends Meeting Friends party." She's terrified by the prospect of meeting his family at the beach. Some of them will be at the cottage.

Spark: I'll look forward to your next report.

Spark: You're not meeting with John?

Spark: John requires no immediate support. He's walking on daisies, he's beaming with joy, he's bursting with energy. He is, in short, an annoyance to everyone around him. Were we together, he would talk only of Emily, which might bring him pleasure but would cover me with tedium.

Spark: I don't believe you. Good evening, Max.

Spark: Bonsoir, mon ange.

Chapter Sixteen

General Report: Max

It was John who dreamed up the "Friends Meeting Friends" party. Unseen by him, I was riding beside him in the car that late afternoon and so was there when it happened. He was driving home from work, talking to Emily on his cell phone. He had just launched into a description of some of his acquaintances, including one with the mysterious moniker of "Rug Rat," when that big goofy grin exploded on his face. He pushed himself erect, his eyes dancing with excitement, and I knew right away the idea that had just popped into his mind was about to pop out of his mouth. At such moments John became a puppy: lively, irrepressible, and witless.

"Let's throw a big party," he said. "Last Saturday of the month. You invite your friends and I'll invite mine."

"Pardon me?" Emily said.

"A get-together of our friends. A party."

"Oh, John. I don't know. I'm not sure that's a good idea."

"It'll be awesome. We'll bring them all together and see what happens."

"That's what I'm afraid of—that we'll see what happens."

"What could go wrong?"

"About a thousand things. One of my friends, Mrs. Schmidt from the apartment building, is seventy-four years old. Should I invite her?"

"Sure. She might enjoy hanging out with young people all night."

"And we'll have this party where?"

"My house, of course. I've got the big living room and the back deck. Even if it rains, I can accommodate thirty, thirty-five people."

"I'll help you clean."

"No, no," said John. "I'll hire a service."

"And the food?"

"I could have it catered."

"Why not go pot-luck? Serve a main course and ask everyone to bring a favorite dish."

"Some of my friends can't even open a can of beans."

"They could buy something at the store. Bringing food makes everyone feel a part of the celebration. Speaking of which, what are we celebrating? Are you going to put anything on the invitation?"

"Just knowing each other."

"I don't think that belongs on the invitation."

"How about our six weeks anniversary?"

"Six weeks doesn't usually call for a grand celebration."

"Six weeks is significant. Getting to six weeks shows a certain level of commitment." When Emily didn't reply right away, John said: "Hey, I know what we can do. You've told me about the Church's feast-days. What's up for Saturday June 28th?"

"Let me look at the calendar." Emily carried the phone to her calendar in the kitchen. "It's the feast of the Immaculate Heart of Mary."

"I don't think that one would go over big with my friends."

"Or some of mine. I don't really think that calls for a party."

"Hey, I know. We'll call it 'Friends Meeting Friends.'"

"'Friends Meeting Friends.'" She paused, and I could imagine the worried look on her face, her fingers twisting her hair. "I like that, John. That sounds nice."

The gleam in his eyes could have illumined a small town.

And so it was settled. A cleaning crew entered John's house and dusted baseboards, polished tables and shelves, passed vacuums over the carpeting, and filled four big black trash bags with debris: old magazines, newspapers, broken electronic equipment, and tattered clothing. Invitations were sent via email and telephone, and thirty-five people, including the withered Mrs. Schmidt, responded positively. (Though he invited Maggie and I to bring some of our own friends, John seemed relieved when we politely declined. "That would spoil the mise-en-scene," I replied, no doubt costing him a minute of precious time Googling the term on his phone). After much debate with himself, John decided to serve both salmon and barbequed pork, dual entrées that seemed most likely to appeal to tastes running from the organic crowd to NASCAR fans. The guests would provide the side dishes and desserts.

With the exception of the invitations sent out by Emily, John prepared the party, overseeing the smallest detail. He became a dervish of activity, spending each evening figuring out what flowers to purchase for the food table, buying vigil candles for placement on end tables and shelves, placing an ashtray on the far corner of the deck in case someone smoked, buying wine and beer at Sam's, and keeping a running tally of the invitations as they arrived. Two days before the party, he took a count and realized he had only sixteen chairs and the sofa for seating. He purchased an additional six white plastic chairs for the deck and hoped that everyone else would be willing to stand or sit cross-legged on the carpet.

The day before the party, with the house clean as a saint's conscience, the chairs carefully placed, the candles awaiting only the touch of a match, the salmon purchased, the barbeque ordered from Twelve-Bones, John prepared himself for his big splash with Emily. His hair was cut, his nails clipped—he considered a manicure, but found that a bridge too far—his outfit of clean white shirt and khaki trousers carefully tucked away in the closet.

John's lavish attention to detail befuddled Emily and Maggie, but his motives were apparent to me. He was performing all of these tasks for the same reasons that men had once crossed swords in battle, or fought dragons, or journeyed to strange and savage lands: to impress a woman. Lacking wars, dragons, and savage shores, John undertook his great labors in hopes of stamping an impression on the woman whom he was rapidly coming to adore. Comrades would not voice his praises, poets would not sing his victory, troubadours would not carry his tale to distant castles to thrill the hearts of lovelorn maidens, but his motive and his actions were nonetheless done in the cause of love. John would be a happy man if Emily alone noticed his efforts.

By seven o'clock that Saturday evening, the "Friends Meeting Friends" party had brought together quite a crew. In addition to Maggie's elderly Mrs. Schmidt, who guzzled beer and smoked Camels, we counted among our guests several teachers from Emily's school; a gay waiter from the champagne bar whom she'd befriended; two women and a man from the French club to which she belonged who at one point sang Edith Piaf songs from the deck; some men and women from John's hiking club; three female employees of the pharmacy; three sets of neighbors; a Russian couple he'd befriended in the pharmacy; and a few of John's sports buddies.

John's party was a success. No guests vomited over the railing of the deck, no major appliances were broken, the salmon, pork, and side dishes were delicious and abundant, and the wine and beer were consumed at a moderate pace. Conversation flowed, and the two groups of friends made some connections. One of John's sports-minded friends, a tall lumbering fellow whom everyone called "Bubba," whose name is apparently derived from the Dixie pronunciation of "brother," secured the phone number of Miranda Hernandez, the slim, dark librarian from Emily's school. Stephen, the homosexual waiter, entertained the neighbors and later the Russians with outrageous stories of his life in Asheville and Boston. The hikers and the Francophiles entered into a long discussion of the countryside of Southern France, and Maggie was entertained for the better part of an hour by a group of women discussing hairstyles.

John was everywhere that evening, pouring drinks, encouraging visits to the buffet, changing out the music on the CD player, sparking conversations and making introductions. Frequently, he cast anxious, covert glances at Emily to see whether she approved of his performance.

With some satisfaction, I noted that she not only approved, but that she seemed in awe of his exuberance and his concern for the welfare of his guests. So did her friends. Out of earshot from Emily, several of them complimented John on his party. They also told him how much they loved Emily and how fortunate he was to have met her. While eating a piece of strawberry yogurt pie, whipped together by, of all people, Bubba, Nina Esolen, a second-grade teacher, complimented Emily to John, adding, with a glint in her eye: "If you hurt her, I'll kill you."

Meanwhile, Emily encountered several of John's friends. They told her they found him a changed man since meeting her, and were amused by the transformation. "He used to look as sad as a hound on a bad night," reported Moose, a small, wiry man whose build was at odds with his name.

Maggie and I had volunteered to help cleanup. Once the guests had departed, and we had gathered stray drinks and disposable plates, the four of us were in the kitchen, where John was washing silverware that Emily dried with a dish towel. John was still high from the party, brokenly whistling Jacques Brel's "Si tu ne me quitte pas," sung by the French crowd, when Emily touched his arm. He looked up from the spatula he was washing, his hands dripping soap and water, and turned sideways as Emily hugged him.

"I love you for what you did tonight," she said. John actually blushed, a deep rubicund glow beneath his tan, and for once was speechless. She kissed him on the lips as if Maggie and I weren't there.

"I love you," she said.

Chapter Seventeen

Recording: Margaret

It is early evening, the Sunday before Independence Day, the day after John's Friends party. Emily and I are sitting on her porch overlooking Cumberland Avenue.

Emily is casually dressed in a denim jumper and a t-shirt, and is bare-footed. She has braided her hair into pigtails, a farm-girl look. She has brought out a pitcher of sweetened iced tea and a plate of sugar cookies. We exchange a few pleasantries about last night's party—she asks me how work is going at the hospital, whether I have pets, and whether I enjoy baking—and then she brings the conversation to John and the impending trip to the coast.

Emily: John has to work Wednesday. We thought we could leave here around eight on Thursday and come home late Sunday. He wanted to drive, but my car has more room for the four of us, and it gets better gas mileage. Could you and Max meet us here?

Margaret: That should work fine. Max will be back in town by then.

Emily: John says it takes about seven hours. (Here occurs a long pause as Emily munches on a cookie and sips her iced tea while gazing intently at two women pushing baby strollers on the sidewalk below the deck. Patience at this point is the name of the game. Emly has the air of a philosopher brooding over some page from Wittgenstein. I munch a cookie and wait for her next words).

Emily: Maggie, I'm totally freaked-out about meeting his parents. His brother and his sister-in-law may come too.

Margaret: Meeting the parents is always tough. They'll judge everything about you, from the way you dress to your opinions on the weather. When they're alone, they'll take you apart detail by detail. They'll dissect you.

Emily: I hope you're joking.

Margaret: Only a little.

Emily: You certainly know how to build a girl's confidence.

Margaret: Listen here, Emily. For one hundred and eighty days of every year you face a classroom of five and six year olds. Don't you realize how much that prospect terrifies some of us who aren't teachers? From what you've told me, you love your students and they love you. You moved up here to get away from your family, to live independently, and you have succeeded. You're a woman of courage and competence. I could give you a pep talk, but I know you'll do just fine.

Emily: So I should just be myself?

Margaret: Well, only to an extent. None of us should really just be ourselves, or we might all end up murdered.

Emily *(laughing)*: True.

Margaret: Be the best you can be, which is great. You'll do fine with John's parents. Has he told you anything about them?

Emily: A little. His dad loves sports and is a big Carolina fan. He owns an insurance agency and has some large investments. His mother comes from money. She has family around Charleston. John says she always dresses up and can't stand disorder or messes. When he was growing up, she was pretty rigid about keeping the house tidy. They had a maid three days a week, and whenever John and his friends came inside, they had to take their shoes off.

Margaret: Like the Japanese?

Emily: I guess so.

Margaret: It does keep dirt out of the house. Are they believers?

Emily: Christians, you mean?

Margaret: Yes.

Emily: I don't think so. They took their children to the Episcopalian Church on Christmas and sometimes at Easter. John says his dad likes to play golf on Sunday mornings and his mother's religion is politics. He said they go at Christmas for the music—his father likes Christmas carols. John once said as a joke that his father believed in golf and money, and his mother believed in the Democratic Party. He said his father supported President Obama because Obama believed in golf and money, and his mother supported him because he was a Democrat.

Margaret: Hmmmm.

Emily: I think they're both pretty materialistic.

Margaret: What's your own family like, Emily?

Emily: Oh, very different. Dad's an electrician who works for a company specializing in hotel and restaurant construction. He's worked all over North and Central Florida. Mom stayed at home taking care of me and my sisters and brother. They were high-school sweethearts and got married after Mom graduated from college. They're both devout in their faith, but without making a fuss about it. Dad's good with his hands—he can build just about anything—and he has a shelf of books on the Seminole Indians, and Mom likes to bargain-hunt and cook. Dad's parents have lived in North Florida for generations, and Mom's family moved to Florida from Western New York when she was a little girl. They have a small house, which was always loud and crowded when I was growing up, but in a good way, if you know what I mean.

Margaret: A home filled with love?

Emily: Exactly. And chaos. (She laughs). I miss it.

Margaret: There's something else, isn't there?

Emily: Well, yesterday John told me his mom had asked him whether I'd be sleeping with him while we were there. Apparently one of the two bedrooms on the first floor is nicer than another and opens onto the beach, and she wanted to know which one he wanted. According to John, she asked him if it was going to be "boy-boy, girl-girl, or girl-boy, girl-boy."

Margaret: Ah. And what did you say?

Emily: I told him I didn't think he and I were ready to sleep together.

Margaret. And what did he say?

Emily: Not too much, but I could tell he wasn't particularly happy about it. And then I thought of you and Max. There is some sort of rec room with a Ping-Pong table and a sofa on the same floor, and if you and Max want your own room, I could sleep there. I'm a good sleeper and I—

Margaret: I assumed you and I would be sharing a room.

Emily: So you and Max aren't sleeping together?

Margaret: Do you mean are we having sex?

Emily: Yes. I don't mean to pry—it's none of my business, I know—but if his mother hadn't brought it up, then—

Margaret: We're not having sex.

Emily: Then we can room together.

Margaret: If I snore, just throw a pillow at my head.

Emily: Same here. (Another long pause). I don't know what to do about the sex part exactly.

Margaret: Your faith again?

Emily: That and common sense. Maybe too much common sense. In college I didn't practice my faith, and I'm not a virgin, but when I came back to the Church I wanted to come back all the way. Only now I've met someone and he's great—no, he's more than great, I love him—and so here I am.

Margaret: It is a dilemma.

Emily: I don't want to be a prude. And I definitely don't want to lose him. But I can feel this attraction growing between us every time he touches me, and he feels it and he's going to want something to happen. He hasn't said as much, but he's a guy, and I'm pretty sure he's had his share of women. If I keep saying no to him—and I'm not sure whether I can keep doing that or if I even want to—then I'm afraid he's going to leave me.

Margaret: It's tricky.

Emily: How do you and Max manage? Or doesn't he pressure you?

Margaret: We've come close. But one of us has always managed restraint. Max more than me, to be truthful.

Emily: Why haven't you?

Margaret: Well, we're both believers. We try and practice our beliefs, no matter how hard it is. And then there's respect, too, I think. We both know something will change if we make love, and we're not sure it would necessarily change for the better. We honor each other by respecting those beliefs. And then there's the mystery, of course.

Emily: What mystery?

Margaret: The mystery of the body and the spirit joined. The mystery of God's presence. The sacramental nature of marriage.

Emily: I've never thought of it that way.

Margaret: Not many people do these days. But it's what God wants.

Emily: I know. I know. And I know it's for the best. I wish John believed that way. You're lucky about Max.

Margaret: I suppose I am. Maybe we can work on John.

Emily: He doesn't hold a very high opinion of Christians, especially fundamentalists. I'm not sure he likes Catholicism much either, but he hasn't said so directly.

Margaret: Does he know anything about the faith?

Emily: No, I'm sure he doesn't. He gets a lot of his ideas from the news, which is awful in terms of the Church, of course. And from his mother—I can't be sure, but from the little he's said about her beliefs she has all sorts of terrible opinions. She's into politics, and whenever religion gets in the way she apparently throws a fit. John's only hinted at these things, but I'm pretty sure he's trying to warn me that I'm about to enter a storm.

Margaret: Maybe I can help calm the waters.

Emily: And Max. He seems to have a nice touch.

Margaret: We'll see.

Chapter Eighteen

Report: Thursday evening: Margaret

Nice touch indeed. Most people on the Fourth of July create explosions using bottle rockets and Roman candles. Max used words.

Our trip to the coast was smooth and easy, and we were in fine spirits as well, until we made that turn into the driveway of the Flyte house. On the highway, we listened to music ranging from Mozart to Randy Newman, swapped stories, and ate with zest the ham sandwiches and apples Emily had packed for our lunch. Once there was an hour or so as we drove through the flat coastal countryside when we quieted, and Emily napped. When he saw she was asleep, John reached out to her and touched her hair and the back of her neck, an endearing gesture—he thought I was asleep too, behind my sunglasses—which spoke well of his feelings for her.

The only disquiet on our journey was sitting beside Max. We held hands a time or two, but we both realized even that small act could take us into dangerous waters. While Max slept, I scrunched sideways and studied him. His head rested against the window of the door, and sleep had relaxed his face, taking away some of the customary stern appearance created by his sharp features. His mouth hung slightly open, like a little boy's. He looked rumpled, cute, precious.

As we crossed the bridge to Emerald Isle, John seemed to have left all his good cheer on the mainland behind us. Gone was the carefree man with a big smile. He grew stiff, sitting erect, both hands gripped on the steering wheel, back and neck straight as a soldier on parade. He failed to laugh at some small joke made by Max, didn't hear my question about the quality of the seafood at Captain Wilcox's Restaurant as we passed it by, and never acknowledged by word or smile Emily's affectionate stroke of his hair. I believe he actually lost his tan and turned two shades paler during that five-mile drive.

When he pulled the car up onto a concrete pad, Max let out a low whistle. "If this is a cottage," he began, but hushed when I threw him a look. I turned to John. "Are you feeling all right, John? You look a little pale."

He had cut the engine, but instead of getting out of the car he stared out the front window as if the sandy beach and the ocean beyond had suddenly turned into hell. "It's my mother," he said, not to me but to Emily. "I should have explained more. She can be—" He paused, rummaging around for the right word, and Max helped him out. "Daunting," he said.

"Yes, daunting."

"Well, let's go see," Max said. "Better daunted than boiled alive."

We clambered from the car into the baking heat and unloaded the bags. Looming before us was a three-story yellow mansion. White shutters trimmed each window, and a manicured lawn lapped at the exterior walls. A magnificent white double staircase, wide at the base and narrowing at the door to which it ran, waited to carry visitors into a vacation paradise.

"In the high season it rents for ten thousand a week," John said. "But my parents keep it for themselves over the Fourth."

We ascended the stairs, already perspiring in the humid air. John was slump-shouldered and silent, as was Emily, who had clearly caught his mood, but Max bounced up the steps. It was he who pushed the doorbell, and a moment later it was he who first entered the house once the maid, whom John called Felicia and kissed on the cheek, had opened the door.

Except for Mr. Flyte, who was, as Felicia explained, napping upstairs in preparation for his evening's golf, the rest of the family was gathered in the great room. Carrying our luggage, we left Felicia to go about her other duties and followed John down a short hallway and through another door into an enormous room. Here was a large kitchen with marble countertops, separated by a bar and stools from the dining area, at the center of which stood a table with twelve chairs. Beyond was an even broader space, its polished wooden floor strewn with oriental rugs, sofas, and chairs, and gleaming with sunlight admitted from glass doors and an enormous skylight. A flat-screen television dominated one wall. Lush ferns called the eye to the fireplace, and shelves of books and movies completed a picture of peaceful ease. The room shouted for repose: the plump sofas demanded naps; the chairs invited you to curl up with a book; the leather-clad stools at the wet bar requested the pleasure of company; the thick, colorful carpets looked more appealing than most beds.

Out of this quiet opulence Mrs. Flyte, her son Steven, and his wife Kristen rose to greet us. They made a handsome trio: Mrs. Flyte tall, unnaturally thin, face bronzed by the sun, wearing a low-cut sundress; Steven, one hand on his hip, the other holding a frosty cocktail glass, his hair curled by the saltwater and his cheeks sporting a day's growth of beard; Kristen still in her two-piece swim suit and a man's unbuttoned white shirt, lithe, brown, blonde. Each emitted that lazy self-confidence engendered by generations of money and power.

After a round of introductions, Mrs. Flyte said: "Your father's napping. Big game of golf early this morning, and he's playing later today. He was all worked up because he played with Jack Dworkin and beat the socks off him. Does anyone need to freshen up? Or a drink? Steven just mixed the best margaritas."

Emily, John, and I shook our heads, but Max opted for a drink. Steven sauntered to the bar and began his work. Emily and John sat on the sofa opposite Mrs. Flyte, while I took a white rocker with cushions and Max sunk into a leather chair. "And you had a pleasant trip down? You made good time."

"Very nice," John said. "We got an early start. That helped."

She swiveled her wicker chair toward Max. "John tells me you're an attorney?"

"I am."

"You have an interesting voice. Were you born here?"

"Oh, yes. But I spent my early years in London. My mother was an attorney there."

"And you're a nurse, Maggie?"

"At Mission-Saint Joe's in Asheville."

"What a lovely town. Fred and I wish we could get up there more often, but things keep coming up. We hardly ever see John." She then turned her attention to Emily. "And your John's new friend? A kindergarten teacher?"

"Yes."

"Interesting. Where do you teach?"

"A Montessori school. Divinum Auxilium Academy."

"That's quite a mouthful for a five year old."

"Yes."

"It's Catholic, I assume?"

"Yes."

"How interesting. And you like it there?"

"I do."

"And you're Catholic?"

"I am, but it's not a requirement. Some of the teachers are Protestant."

"Are you from Asheville originally?"

"No. Florida. The Gainesville area."

"Interesting. And you have siblings?"

"A sister and three brothers."

"A big family these days. Interesting."

Her use of "interesting" was barbed with innuendo. She sipped her drink. "Kristen's from Florida, too. Jacksonville. She and Steven met in college at Chapel Hill. Fred was there to play golf, met Kristen's dad, who was there for the same reason, and they took the kids out to supper. Do you golf?"

"No, I never have."

"And your parents work?"

"My dad's an electrician. My mom works at home."

"Very interesting." She chatted a minute or two about some electric repairs done to the house and the hot tub. Then she said to Emily, "Please excuse all my questions, but John's been very secretive about you. Usually when he finds a girl he's absolutely full of himself. Remember Leah from Spartanburg, dear? I've forgotten her last name—Hobson? Higgins?"

"Henson."

"Ah, yes. Leah Henson. Anyway, John talked about her with me on the phone, though I never met her, and he sounded very excited. They golfed and played tennis together. I remember she even shared his addiction to video games. How long did you see her, John? A couple of years?"

"Not quite a year." John shifted his feet, glanced at Emily, then said to his mother: "Maybe we should move the bags into our rooms."

"In a minute. We'll finish these drinks—Max has just started his—and then we'll help you get settled. Anyway, Emily, you come to us as a mystery. John has told us almost nothing about you."

"I hope we'll get to know each other this weekend," Emily said, softly. With each of Mrs. Flyte's remarks, she had moved nearer John, as if seeking shelter. It was an endearing sight, but I wished she wasn't quite so shy.

But now it was Kristen who spoke. "We were discussing the upcoming election. It's an exciting time, isn't it?"

"Lots at stake this fall," Max said. "Do you have a horse in the race?"

"We're all huge supporters of the president. So of course we hope the Democrats hold the Senate."

"Mother works quite a bit in Raleigh for the Democratic Party," Steven said. "And I'm helping a candidate running for State Senate."

"The president has to win," Mrs. Flyte said. "If he loses, it means the end of all the changes he's made."

"I wasn't aware he was running," Max said.

"His party is. And if the party loses, you'll see people poorer than ever. "

"'The poor will be with us always,'" Max said.

"They will be if the Republicans have their way," Steven said. "Where did you get that anyway? Ronald Reagan?"

"For God's sakes, Steven," Mrs. Flyte said. "It's from the Bible. Moses, wasn't it?"

"It's true, though, isn't it," Max said, ignoring her faux pas. He was lounging back in one of the fat cushioned chairs as if he hadn't a care in the world. "People will never be equal. Different talents, different aspirations. Some will always have less or more than others."

"But we can help those who are poor," Mrs. Flyte said.

"Certainly," Max said. "And we should help the truly poor. But poor in America is different than poor in, say, Calcutta. Here the poor have cell phones, televisions, cables, and computers. No one starves. It's a very different standard. We've created an enormous underclass of people who seem permanently stuck in place."

"But the government has to help them. Some of them can't make do otherwise. Without charity they couldn't survive."

"Charity never comes at the point of a gun."

"Gun? Gun?" said Steven. It was then I realized he was drunk. To be charitable, I must add that he had just come in off the beach, that he may have neglected eating lunch, and that the combination of sun, tequila, and an empty stomach might send the hardiest barfly reeling. "How do guns get into the discussion?"

"Try not paying your taxes," Max said, "and you'll find out."

"I do pay my taxes. I'm proud to pay my taxes. I am in favor of higher taxes, especially on fat-cat corporations."

"I've never liked guns," Kristen said. She wasn't drunk, I don't think, but the brightness in her eyes and voice was artificial. She was high on something other than liquor. "The government should take guns away. Do you know how many people are killed by guns every year in this country?"

"Not off-hand," Max said. "How many?"

"A lot. A whole shit-load of people. And children too."

"I have a gun," John interrupted in a conversation that struck me as quickly descending into bedlam. "I bought it last year. A Sigma nine millimeter."

"You wouldn't know what to do with it," Steven said.

"I've gone to the range every other week for a year. I'm a tolerable marksman. I can take it apart and put it back together in the dark. I think I'd know what to do with it."

"What's a Sigma nine millimeter?" asked Mrs. Flyte.

"It's a handgun," John said.

"That's weird, John," Kristen said. "I don't see you as a gun owner."

"I like shooting. I even earned my concealed carry permit."

"You have the gun on you right now?"

"It's in my suitcase."

"How strange," said Mrs. Flyte. "I wish you wouldn't bring it into the house."

"Every year children die from guns," Steven said, slurring his words. "The government needs to ban them."

"More children die in swimming pools," Max said. "Perhaps we should ban those."

"If everyone would just support the president's policies, think what a different country this would be," Mrs. Flyte said. "We could take care of the sick, help the poor, better the education of our children, and bring peace to the world."

"This president wants power, not justice," Max said, carelessly. "If he were given his head, the country would become a hell-hole. And then, once we were totally broke, we would become a penurious hell-hole."

I couldn't understand him, his motive in goading the Flyte family. He was perfectly relaxed, leaning back, holding his drink at rest on his chest, legs stretched out with his feet crossed. What was he thinking? Didn't he see he was throwing gasoline over open flames?

"This president is a brilliant man who could save the country if we'd let him."

"This president is a prevaricator and a narcissist."

This comment fell like a brick in the discussion. For a moment I thought Mrs. Flyte, whose mouth had opened as if someone had punched her in the belly, might collapse on the floor. But Steven stepped up with some more gasoline. "Name one of his policies you don't like."

"In Illinois, when he was a state senator, he voted for partial-birth abortion," Max said. "I'd start with that one. To support sticking a sharp instrument through the head of a partially delivered baby and then sucking out the brains tells us something about a person, wouldn't you say?"

"That's nonsense," Mrs. Flyte said, her voice hoarse and raspy. "Sheer nonsense."

"Is it? Look at his record."

Mrs. Flyte stared at Max as if he were a roach on the carpet. Then, inexplicably, she turned to Emily. "What do you think?"

Emily looked at her a moment, square in the eye. She must have seen something disturbing in that glacial face, for she shook her head and looked at the floor. "I don't think we should talk politics. It's—"

"No, I want to know what you think. You teach young children. You have a part, however small, in the direction of this country. What do you think of the president?"

"Well, Max is right about the president's stand on partial birth abortion. He did cast that vote. And his health plan has flaws. I don't think a mandated national healthcare plan should cover contraception. The Church teaches—"

"What church?"

"The Catholic Church."

"My God, young woman, it's the twenty-first century. We left the Dark Ages a long time ago."

"Dark Ages or not," I said forcefully, "the health care mandate forces citizens to pay for procedures that violate their religious beliefs. It forces them to sin or to pay penalties."

With a look of astonishment, Mrs. Flyte turned to me. "You're Catholic, too?"

"As the Pope," I replied, tartly. Her wondering stare—what sort of menagerie had her son brought home?—might have made me smile, but I now understood what Max must have seen from the first: Mrs. Flyte had felt an immediate and instinctive dislike for the three of us. Some intuition in her shrunken soul, some sixth sense found in those who truly despise this world and work like termites to create a utopia of their own imagining, had nosed out our natures.

She turned again to Emily. "Surely you use contraception yourself?"

"Mother," John said. "I don't think—"

"It's just a question. Woman to woman. Let Emily speak for herself. What do you do about sex?"

Emily raised her head, and I saw she had tears in her eyes. "My sexual life is none of your business, ma'am. But since you asked, no, I don't use birth control. I think contraception is wrong. I think couples should wait until marriage and then be open to the possibility of children. I know it's unpopular to think this way, but I—well, I think it's the truth."

For a moment the room grew very still. Mrs. Flyte blinked once. She was smiling now, and I could almost feel her mind turning, letting different tumblers fall into place before unlocking her next remarks. I was certain she would have the grace to turn to another topic. But I was wrong.

Instead, she looked at her son. "John, do you hear this? This Catholic stuff? Did you know about this?"

That Mrs. Flyte kept up this furious line of questioning, that she was deliberately provoking argument, gave me my first hint that she, too, may have visited the margarita pitcher too many times.

John put his arm around Emily and looked at his mother. "No more, Mom," he said. Steven started to interrupt, but John held out a hand against him. "No more from either of you. You have no right—you have no right at all—to treat a guest this way. And I'll work out my own sex life, thank you very much. I don't need your advice or yours—" he pointed to Steven—"on my relationship with Emily. And one more thing: do you see this woman here, Mom? Do you see her? Well, get a good look at her because you know something? She just may be the woman I marry some day. So you better get used to her."

Before anyone else could speak, he turned to Max and me. "Grab your bags and meet me at the car. We're leaving."

"You just got here," Mrs. Flyte said. "You can't leave."

"Watch me," John said.

He took Emily by the arm, guided her across the shining floor, stopped to pick up their luggage, and disappeared into the hall. The door opened and closed.

Max swirled his drink in his glass, drained it, placed it carefully on the coaster on the coffee table, and got to his feet. "Well, that ended badly, didn't it?" he said. "I do thank you all for the refreshments. By the way, Steven, those margaritas could use a touch more Cointreau."

Chapter Nineteen

Private File: Maximilian

"What were you thinking?" Maggie whispered to me as we descended the long, sun-struck staircase to the car. (Whispered is too soft a word; hissed is more accurate).

"Shhhh. Not now," I whispered back, and crossed the concrete pad, still in my mood of jolly swaggering savagery. Emily and John had already stowed their luggage in the trunk, and he was embracing her beside the car while she wept. I dropped my duffel with the other bags, put Maggie's bags on top, and closed the trunk. Then I went round the other side of the car and opened the door on the passenger side. "I'll drive," I said to John. "You two sit in back."

John handed over the keys, helped Emily into the car, which by this point had become an oven, and clambered in beside her. I held the front door open for Maggie, who glared at me as she ducked her head to enter the car, and then went round to the driver's side and started the car. I looked again toward the top of the steps, but as I suspected, no one came flying out of the house to protest our departure. I backed the car up and pulled onto Ocean Drive.

"I'm so sorry," Emily said, wiping at her eyes with the tips of her fingers. "I don't know what I did, but I must have done something. She hated me. I could feel it as soon as she saw me."

She was, of course, absolutely correct. As soon as we had stepped into the great room, the animosity became palpable—not just toward Emily, but toward all of us, including John. That enmity was a thick, black cloud poisoning the air. You could almost smell it.

"It wasn't you, Em," John said. "It wasn't any of you." He paused, then continued: "My family and I have a complicated relationship. I should have explained it. I should have told you about them before we came. And I should have explained about the drinking. I just kept hoping this might be one of their better days. They all drink too much except for Kristen, who uses pills more than liquor."

I had suspected as much. She was as glazed as a pot, but had scarcely touched her drink whereas the other two had almost emptied their glasses.

"Dad was napping because he'd spent a couple of hours at the clubhouse bar after his game. Mom usually shows more control, but Steven has gotten worse these last two years. He lives in her shadow—he works for Dad, and can't stand it, but he's too weak and afraid to change. I'm awfully sorry. I've ruined our trip."

I wanted to reassure John that he had no cause for sorrow on our part. In fact, he had done himself proud. From what he had told me, this was one of the few times in his life he had stood up to his mother's guff. Even more, he had defended Emily. Given his nature, accustomed as he was to abandoning himself and the awful conflicts of his life to toys and games, he had taken a giant step toward manhood. He just didn't know it yet.

While the three of them tried to pick apart what had just happened—Maggie had turned in her seat to face them, though she shot a look at me now and again as if to verify my sanity—I got the car out onto the main highway and drove back in the direction we'd come an hour earlier. We were approaching the island's tip when I saw the office for Blue Water Realty and Rentals off to the left. I turned sharply, pulled into the lot nearest the street, parked beneath the shade of a tree, and rolled down the windows. By then the others had stopped talking and were watching me.

"Wait here," I said. "I'll only be a few minutes."

And a few minutes were all I needed. When I rounded the building and was out of sight of the car, I checked my wallet and found what I expected: several hundred dollars. Some negotiations ensued in the office, a phone call was made, and I signed a lease. When I got back in the car, I handed Maggie a small plastic pouch containing two keys and a standard brochure describing cleanup procedures and checkout times. "We're at the beach, and I need a holiday," I said. "The beachfront houses are all taken, and I couldn't have afforded one anyway, but I did manage to rent us a fifth floor condominium five miles down the road with a balcony overlooking the ocean."

The three of them stared at me as I started the car and pulled from the lot. Taking advantage of their shock and silence, I said: "We'll need provisions. We passed a Food Lion on our way in. There are gas grills available at the condo. Steak and salad would taste delicious this evening. Or do you prefer seafood?'

"I can't let you do that," John said.

"Do what?"

"Pay for the condo."

"You can pay half."

"We're staying here?" Emily said. She was still shell-shocked, her thoughts back in the mansion with Mrs. Flyte cannonading her self-respect.

"We came to the beach," I said. "Let's enjoy ourselves."

Maggie was shaking her head. "You are something else."

"Yes, I know."

She laughed at my allusion and looked fondly at me. Inside the Food Lion, the four of us shopped, filling the cart with everything from tomatoes and fresh spinach to dishwashing liquid and a watermelon. "I'm sure we've forgotten something," I said, "but we can make another run tomorrow. At any rate, I don't think we'll go hungry tonight."

A short drive back down Emerald Isle, a few trips moving luggage and groceries up and down an elevator, and we found ourselves in a tidy two-bedroom condominium with a small kitchen, a spacious living room, and a small terrace. We offered Maggie and Emily the bedroom closer to the ocean—their window looked down onto a wide glittering beach, sun-bathers, and blue water—and John and I took the one on the other side of the shared bath.

By the time we'd unpacked and dressed in bathing suits and sandals, the dark clouds from our visit with the Flytes were dissipating. John came out of the bedroom grinning and dressed for the beach, pointed at me, and said, "You da man, Max. You da man." Maggie kept throwing me glances of incredulity and shaking her head. Even Emily, despite her battering, wore a tentative smile as we headed down the elevator and onto the beach.

The water was tolerably warm, and the sun by then was too low to bother with lotion. The surf washed away the awful remnants of the afternoon, and we splashed about, throwing water at one other and letting the waves burst on us. After half an hour or so, Emily and John toweled off and set off hand in hand for a walk at the water's edge.

"And now you," Maggie said. She shook water from her ears, hopping on one leg, and gripped my hand. "You have some explaining to do."

She dragged me like a convict to the towels, pushed me down on one, and threw another to me for drying myself. When she had finished dabbing away water, she spread the towel and sat opposite me.

"So tell me everything or I'll bury you in sand."

"Everything? What do you mean?"

"Don't play coy with me, buster. Why did you act so terribly at the Flyte's house?"

"Mrs. Flyte didn't think my acting was terrible."

She pulled up a handful of sand and threw it on my leg. "I want answers."

"Be more specific and I'll give them."

"Why did you behave as you did?"

"Because twice John has dropped strong hints that he's become an outcast in the eyes of his family. He alluded to major problems without being specific. And of course, as soon as we entered the room I knew they'd been drinking."

"How could you possibly know that?"

"First, they all had the look in their eyes. Do you know the look I mean?"

She shook her head. Some loose hair, damp with seawater, brushed both sides of her face, and she tucked the strands behind her ears. That gesture brought me up, made me lose my train of thought, and I wondered once again about the object of this exercise. Why were we still together, Maggie and I?

Maggie snapped her fingers at me. "Max, what in heaven's name is wrong with you? I'm waiting."

"Sorry. They all had that look as if they weren't quite present. And Steven was a dead give-away. He's athletic, like John, but he moved with a false dignity when he made my drink. And then when Mrs. Flyte began questioning Emily the way she did, I figured I'd ratchet up the situation to see what would happen."

"Well, that didn't go too well, did it?"

"I thought it went extraordinarily well. Do you know that was one of the few times in his life John has stood up to her? And he did it defending Emily. For once he was a lion instead of a lamb—and from the little he's told me, that's an insult to the courage of lambs. I was proud of him. If we've done nothing else, we've helped John put some iron in his spine."

Maggie held one hand over her eyes, blocking the sun and looking down the beach, and I turned to follow her gaze. Emily and John were a good distance off, standing at the surf's edge and holding hands.

"What do you suppose they're talking about?"

"His mother, of course. His family life. Politics as high religion. He is undoubtedly telling her at this very moment that what happened two hours ago wasn't her fault, but his for not giving her fair warning. He will explain that he brought her here hoping for the best. Soon he will ask her to look beyond his family at him. 'That's my family,' he'll say. 'It's not me.' And then we shall see."

"See what?"

"Whether he has convinced her. The quality of her mercy. She'll be measuring her family against his, and then looking at him. She'll be thinking how much she likes him right now—maybe even loves him—but she'll also be rolling over in her mind that old saying that when you marry someone you marry the family. What's her family like, by the way?"

"Different in nearly every way possible."

'How so?"

"They don't have nearly as much money. They have more children. They struggle and fight just like most people, but they're bound together by love and affection for one another. Alcohol is for special occasions—a sign of festivity. The other evening she told me about her mom and dad, her sister and brothers, and the fondness in her voice was like sunshine. They're also believers. She comes from a very different background than John. It makes me wonder whether they're truly meant for each other. Are we doing the right thing?"

"We're doing what we were sent to do, getting Emily and John acquainted and serving as their example. That's all we know and all we need to know. Besides, as I've said before, love is a little like politics; it brings together strange bedfellows. For example, once I was sent to watch a man and a woman and pray over them. Each was married to another. Both were believers. Both had children and sterling reputations. Both had known each other for a long time. He owned a land surveying business and she was the librarian at the private school her children had once attended. Anyway, one day they ran into each other in a Starbuck's and had a coffee together. Soon they were meeting for coffee or taking walks on a regular basis. Early one evening they arranged to meet for a talk in a garden. It was chilly, and the man offered the woman his coat. As they sat together, side by side against the cold, she raised her face to look at him, and he kissed her."

"Oh."

"Yes. Oh."

"Like Dante's Francesca and Paolo!"

"A little, maybe. Only they never became lovers. There were too many hedges keeping them apart. They wanted each other, but were tormented by the fear of discovery and hurting so many others who loved them."

"What finally happened to them?"

"They called an end to their relationship. They stopped getting together or chatting online. They recognized how much they were tearing themselves apart. But they remained tormented, especially when they saw each other."

"How awful."

"In terms of attraction, love doesn't play by a set of fixed rules. People may be programmed toward attraction—the color of someone's eyes, the cut of the face, the sound of the voice—but then, I think, love for human beings takes all sorts of twists and turns. It's like the old fairy tales humans tell. For example, I can easily imagine a comely woman falling in love with a frog of a man because of his sense of humor. She begins to love him because he makes her laugh."

"Like us, you mean?"

"Vixen," I said, but then paused because she wasn't laughing. Indeed, Maggie looked deadly serious. "Am I really ugly?"

Now she did smile, but faintly. "Max, you're the most beautiful man I've ever seen."

"You're on your first mission, so I'll have to take that compliment with a grain of salt. And I'd prefer handsome to beautiful, by the way."

"Why are we here, Max?"

"To give Emily support. To help John find his way."

"No, I mean why are we here the way we are."

"You've asked me that before."

"I know. But I keep thinking about it. There are other ways of bringing them together."

"I think we're meant to provide them with an example. But that's not what you're asking, is it?"

"No."

"Then all I can come up with is that we're some sort of experiment. As I've told you, I've come as a manifestation many times, but what we are experiencing together has never happened before. Maybe we're supposed to feel what they feel when they fall in love. We've known how it feels to eat, to breathe, to touch. I can still recollect the first time I tasted quesadilla and the explosion of sensations in my mouth. I can remember the first time I smelled a forest at dawn and felt dew on my skin. I can remember the music made by a whippoorwill, and the orchestra of crickets and cicadas on a hot summer's night in Mississippi. But none of us, to the best of my knowledge, has ever truly felt what humans must feel in their hearts: triumph, despair, love, hate. Maybe you and I are supposed to learn something about those things."

"Surely not despair."

"It may be the deadliest of sins, but for some poor souls despair eats at hearts and minds like a worm."

"I'm not sure I want to learn what they feel."

"Nor I, but here we are."

Maggie looked so woebegone that I touched her cheek. We were sitting now knee to knee on the towel—she had slipped a pink t-shirt over her green bathing suit—and she pressed her cheek against the palm of my hand. In a moment she took my hand, held it in her lap, and kissed my lips. Her face and hair smelled of salt and sunshine. Then she smiled and scooted round beside me and putting one arm round my waist, rested her head on my shoulder.

Together we sat and watched the sea.

Chapter Twenty

Report: Public file: Margaret

That evening, Max and John cooked steaks, potatoes, and corn on the cob on the grill in the recreation area beside the condominium while Emily and I prepared the salad. We ate supper on the balcony at twilight. Below us on the beach other vacationers—families with children, a gaggle of teenagers—were setting off holiday fireworks a day early. Cries of delight rose to us as Roman candles, sparklers, and something John called "whiz-bangs" lit up the night. When that particular excitement died away, and after we had stacked plates and glasses in the dishwasher, we opened another bottle of wine, returned to the balcony, and talked until after midnight.

Going to our separate bedrooms provided some humor. Max and John escorted us to the door of our room, lightly offered a goodnight kiss, and retired to their own quarters. Once Emily and I had prepared ourselves for sleep—I gave her the double and took the twin—we lay and talked for a while. She had opened the window, and the wind from the ocean carried the sound of the surf to us in the night.

After a long pause I thought perhaps she had fallen asleep, but then she sighed.

"Still awake, I take it?"

I could hear her rustling in the sheets. When I looked at her, I could see by the moonlight she had propped herself up on her elbow. "When we walked down the beach today, John told me more about his family. His mother and father are both divorced—Steven is from the previous marriage, which may explain why he sides with his mother—and they've both become heavy drinkers over the last ten or fifteen years. John says when he was small, they were happier—or at least that's how he remembers them. Now they both drink and stay angry about politics, his mother more than his father, and play golf."

"It sounds horrid."

"He says they have good days as well as bad, and he was hoping this would be one of their good days. But even on their good days, he says, they can be abrasive toward everyone around them. He says Kristen puts up with it because of the money and because of Steven, and Steven puts up with it because of fear."

"But John doesn't?"

"He did until he went to college. After pharmaceutical school he just couldn't take the stress and anger anymore. He said he had to get away or he'd be just like Steven."

I sat up to look at her. "What did you say?"

"I told him I was sorry. I told him I thought he was brave for taking a stand. I told him I hoped he could still find love for his family in his heart. And I told him I would keep them all in my prayers."

Her comment about prayer roused my curiosity. "How did John react to your offer of prayer?"

"He said his family could use all the prayers they could get. He wasn't saying it to be funny, though, the way people do. He meant it. And then he asked me what it was like to pray. 'I don't understand it,' he said. 'What do you do?'"

"So what did you say, Emily?"

"I told him I could show him better than tell him. I said it was best if you can find some silence—not just make silence around you, but find it in your mind. I told him he could speak if he wanted, but that the best thing was to be patient and quiet, and try to empty your mind enough to let God come inside. Then I held his hands and prayed with him."

I laughed and lay my head on my pillow, facing her and smiling. "That was a good answer."

"Why did you laugh?"

"I was thinking the teacher now has a new pupil. In my mind I saw John sitting with your kindergarteners."

She was quiet again, and I closed my eyes and was nearly asleep when she asked: "What do you think of John?"

"He's bright and fit. He has a good job he likes and the work helps other people. And he has a good soul. But I do think he needs a teacher." I thought a moment, then added: "A teacher just like you."

General report: Maximilian

Sleep carried its usual terror and exhilaration. For all human beings, this passage into unconsciousness, this diminution of the senses, arriving for some with ease, for others only with the aid of a drug, occurs periodically and is not thought unnatural. For creatures like Maggie and me, however, who by nature have no eyes to close or bodies to restore, the loss of control brought by sleep is a uniquely odd sensation. It is a little death, a cessation of consciousness.

Rising from the darkness of sleep is equally strange. Usually when I wake as a manifestation I feel as if I am swimming toward light and air from some great depth in a dark ocean, pulling with my arms and kicking my legs to reach the faraway sun-lit surface.

When I opened my eyes on this particular morning, light from the new dawn was just touching the windows of our room. We had left the curtains open, and in the grey luminescence I saw John standing at the window, still dressed in the boxer shorts and t-shirt he'd worn to bed. His hair stuck up in several places from sleep, and his face was raw with confusion.

"Heavy thoughts?"

He jerked at the sound of my voice and turned to me. "You're awake."

"What time is it?"

"Almost six."

"Been up long?"

He shook his head. "Not too long. I may try and catch some more sleep in a few minutes."

I kicked at the sheet and bedcovers, which had become tangled around my legs, and sat up in bed. "Everything okay?"

"I was just thinking about yesterday. That was a good thing you did, renting this place. It gave us a second chance at some fun. I wish I'd thought of it."

"You were a trifle preoccupied with other events at the time."

"Still—" His voice faded. He left the window and sat on the edge of his own bed. "I want to apologize again for what happened. Usually I can handle them better than I did. But when Mom started in on Emily—and believe me, she was just warming up—I lost it."

"You were right to defend Emily. Your mother was wrong to attack her. There's nothing to apologize for." I stretched out and lay sideways, regarding him. John Flyte had traveled a good distance in the last twenty-four hours, and he didn't quite know what to make of the trip. "What's your father like?"

"Dad? He's okay, though when I was a kid he never had much time for me. I don't blame him for that—he was working hard—but I do wish he'd been around more. Being around my mother was intense and stressful for him—she has some high expectations—but even that was bearable. But they both kept drinking more and more over the years, and they cut out everyone but themselves. Don't get me wrong—they had lots of acquaintances, and in the summer other family would visit, but home was a cold place for Steven and me." He stopped a moment, then said: "I actually feel sorry for Steven. He's bright, brighter than he came across yesterday, and he picked a good girl when he married Kristen. But between trying to please my parents and the drinking and the drugs, they're both as trapped in their lives as my parents are."

"A steep ditch."

"Very steep." He shook his head. "Poor Steven. Anyway, when I decided to become a pharmacist, the announcement caused a big stink. I broke the news at home over Christmas break my freshman year and we spent the rest of the vacation fighting about it. When I went back to school, I made a vow never to become like them and to spend as little time as possible at home."

"What made you want to become a pharmacist?"

"It's funny how many people ask me that. If I'd become a doctor—that's what Mom wanted when she realized how interested I was in science—everyone would have celebrated. Anyway, I loved science, and the idea that medicines and pills and vitamins could have such an effect on the body fascinated me. Still does, in fact." He laughed. "Maybe my parents' drinking influenced me in that regard. Their drug of choice has certainly had an effect."

"Why not research, then?"

"I don't have the personality, or for that matter, the brains. I've participated in a few projects. Once, right after graduation, I went as a sort of hired hand on a field trip to Mexico to look at some different natural drugs. I was out of my depth. Plus, to be frank, I wanted to make some money right away. Research would have meant another three or four years of graduate school with no guarantees of employment after finishing."

"That sounds sensible."

"Maybe. Or just greedy." He paused in recollection, looking at some invisible point on the wall beyond me. "Growing up, I had too much money and way too many things, and I got away with stuff all the time. My mom and dad gave me everything but themselves." That invisible point must have disappeared, for he looked at me again. "Anyway, that was the year I started to change, to take some interest in work instead of play. I still have too many things, too many toys, but I also work hard now. They're mine—they weren't given to me. And now—well, now I look at Emily and see someone who's actually good. Someone who adores her family, who's doing something that really counts in the long run. Emily's like that Christmas break was for me—a wake-up call."

"How so?"

"This will probably sound stupid, but she makes me want to be better than I am."

"One of the many purposes of women."

John laughed, and some of the tightness left his face. "I suppose that's true. She's the sort of person you can count on to do the right thing—or at least try to do the right thing. The way she behaved yesterday at my parents' house—she was trying to make them happy without giving up herself in the process. That's exactly where Steven and Kristen have gone off track. They gave up too much of themselves, and they've filled in the holes with booze and pills."

"You did pretty well yourself yesterday."

"You think so? Well, maybe I did. I'm certain Mom was surprised. That part about marriage—I don't even know where that came from. I think that surprised Emily."

"You can count on it," I said, remembering her face when John had announced his intentions. "Did she mention it later?"

"No. And I first thought maybe she didn't hear it with all the emotions flying around. But now I'm pretty sure she did. It's nothing I can put a finger on—she just looks at me in a different way."

"Oh, she heard it."

"How do you know?"

"I saw it in her eyes."

John smiled, and his face filled with the dreamy gratitude of a Labrador retriever who has just received a long-awaited pat on the head. Then he sat on the bed, yawned, and stretched out. "I might try to catch some more sleep. If we get up before them, maybe we could make breakfast."

"Sounds good."

I closed my eyes and drifted again into the shadows of sleep.

When next I woke, it was to the scent of coffee and bacon. After pulling on shorts and sandals, and brushing my teeth, I followed this perfume into the kitchen, where John stood wearing an apron against the spitting bacon. In the adjacent dining area the table was set with silverware, napkins, four orange juices, and coffee mugs.

"Smells delicious."

"Did I wake you?"

"No, and even if you had, there's no better lure than bacon and coffee. Are the girls up yet?"

"Haven't heard a thing. I wanted to surprise them."

"I think you've surprised us all."

Just then came the click of a latch and the door opened. Maggie came out, dressed in a loose smock hiding her bathing suit. Behind her was Emily, similarly attired and with an enormous smile. "I can't believe you did this," she said, glancing at the table and then back at John. "You guys are great."

"It was all John," I said. "I've just come out myself."

"You did this?"

"I wanted to make sure you kept your strength up. We're facing a long hard day of lying on the beach, reading books, and walking the surf."

She moved to him and into his arms, kissed him on the lips, and then hugged him. "I've always loved a man in an apron."

John blushed, but Emily just laughed again, kissed him, and put her head against his chest as if all eternity had prepared her to do so.

Chapter Twenty-One

Report: Public file: Margaret

Our three days at the beach have done wonders for Emily and John.

We quickly and naturally hit a schedule. John prepared enormous breakfasts of eggs, bacon or sausage, toast, and fruit, after which we would go down to the beach until eleven or so, when the temperature, even under the umbrellas, became too hot for comfort. We ate a light lunch—crackers, cheese, apples, and melons—and spent the afternoons inside reading or talking. Around three we returned to the sand and water, where we splashed in the ocean or lay beneath the sun or sat just beyond the breaking waves on the rafts John had bought from the nearby convenience store. In the evenings we took turns preparing suppers, then took long strolls in the moonlight along the surf followed by board games around the table in the dining area. By midnight we had usually tumbled into bed, where Emily and I might talk for a few minutes more about any number of topics—men, her family, her dreams of the future—before falling into a sleep made heavy by salt and sun.

Max and I performed well. We answered any questions they asked about our past, deftly turning the answers into questions or deflecting their attention to another topic. We followed our instructions to provide them with an example, showing each other every consideration, offering encouragement and innocent physical affection.

On Saturday evening we attended the Mass at Saint Mildred's in Swansboro. Afterwards, while John and Emily prepared supper together—he had bought oysters and some shrimp, and Emily was preparing a rice casserole in which she specialized—I could hear him peppering her once more with questions about the Mass and her faith. His ignorance was vast, but Emily had schooled herself well in Church teaching after coming back to the faith.

"So there's a structure to the whole thing," John said. "First there's the general confession, then asking for mercy, then prayers, the readings, the Creed, the bread and wine, and the end."

"It starts as bread and wine, but it becomes the body and blood of Christ."

"That's the part I have trouble understanding," John said. (I was happy with his tone. He and Emily were now comfortable enough together so that he could bring up a topic without feeling as if he was walking on tiptoe). "The priest says some words and the bread and wine become flesh and blood. Do people really believe that?"

"He doesn't just say words. He says the words Christ said and told us to say. And not everybody who goes to Mass believes it, which is sad."

"But you believe it?"

"I try." She hesitated, then said: "Yes, I believe."

"That you're really eating flesh and blood?"

"Not human flesh and blood. The flesh and blood of Christ."

"But don't you mean it's a symbol?"

"No. Have you ever read Flannery O'Connor?"

"Didn't he play for the Red Sox a while back?"

Both Max and I were sitting in the living room, and smiled at each other when John asked this question. It was all I could do not to burst into laughter.

Emily may have felt the same urge, but all she said was: "No, silly, Flannery O'Connor is a she, not a he, and she wrote novels and short stories. Her short stories are the best. Anyway, once she was having supper somewhere and one of the other writers at the table said the Eucharist was just a symbol and Flannery O'Connor got mad and said, 'Well, if it's a symbol, then to hell with it.'"

"What'd she mean by that?"

"She meant the Host was the body of Christ or it was nothing."

They went on in this vein for a few more minutes, with John asking why the priest couldn't marry, why the altar servers processed with candles, why there was a statue of a woman near the altar, and a dozen other questions. Emily acquitted herself well, never laughing at his ignorance, and several times, I am quite certain, pausing in her explanations to kiss him.

After supper Max and I offered to wash the dishes and tidy the kitchen while Emily and John took a blanket and went for a walk on the beach.

Report: Private file: Maximilian

We rinsed the plates, glasses, and flatware, and loaded them into the dishwasher, and then Maggie scrubbed the few pans and pots in the sink while I wiped down the dining room table. When I came back into the kitchen carrying the damp sponge and a paper towel containing some bits of debris left from supper, she was just finishing up, bent over the sink and unaware of my presence.

The back of her neck stopped me in the doorway. This evening she had foregone her usual braid, instead piling up her hair into a loose bun. Exposed, slightly moist with her exertions and with the steamy water, the back of her neck was, I thought, extraordinarily beautiful. For the moment I acquired the eye of an artist, a painter, and in those few inches of flesh, muscle, bone, and nerve I found an object of erotic desire. I wanted to kiss that tanned neck and the side of her throat; I wanted to breath in her perfume of sun, salt, and tanning oil; I wanted to trace her lovely, ruddy face with my fingers. The wine I'd been drinking—I had just freshened our glasses—was not the cause for this urge, nor was it the sunshine we'd built up inside ourselves that day, that sensation produced by a long day of salt and warmth when the human body wants to burst like a grape with carnality. No—these were trifles. It was Maggie herself I desired.

Maggie must have felt me watching her, for she turned and smiled at me, then looked more intently into my eyes and blushed. She was wearing a white sleeveless shift that gave an even deeper sheen to the tan on her arms and throat, and I felt weak from my desire to touch her. Slowly she turned back to the sink, pulled the plug to release the water, dried her hands on a towel hanging from the oven handle, and wiped at the counter beside the sink with a sponge. Still she didn't look at me, and I wondered whether she might be angry at my fracturing of the unspoken vow we'd taken to steer away from passion. But then she carefully squeezed out the sponge, rinsed her hands, dried them again on the towel, picked her glass of wine from the counter, and said in a low voice: "Why don't you bring your wine out on the balcony?"

She left the kitchen, and I threw away the mess I'd brought from the dining room and got my glass of wine and the bottle. I took another minute straightening up the chairs around the table and arranging the placemats. When I came out onto the balcony, she had made up a sort of pallet there from the beach towels we'd hung to dry earlier that day. She'd pushed the chairs and small table to one side, and was waiting for me, sitting on the towels, drinking her wine, staring at the beach and the stars through the porch railing.

"Why were you looking at me that way in the kitchen?" she asked after I'd sat beside her.

She whispered the words. Between the balconies of the condominiums were stucco walls, which concealed sight but not sound from the neighbors.

To tell her that I had momentarily fallen in love with her neck seemed foolish, and was partially untrue in the bargain—I loved more than that lovely nape of neck—but I whispered the truth: "I was admiring your neck and—"

Maggie giggled. "My neck? Isn't it a neck like all necks?"

"No, it's strong and finely shaped, and at the time it was glistening with a hint of perspiration. But it's not just your neck."

"What then?"

"I love you, Maggie. I can't help it."

"But what about our agreement?"

"Le coeur a ses raisons, que le raison ne connait point."

"Pascal again?"

"Pascal. The heart has its reasons which reason cannot know."

"That adage gives rise to many of the problems in this world."

"Agreed. But there is truth in it."

"I wish there were directions. Regarding us, I mean."

I scooted closer to her, until our knees were touching. "Listen," I said. "Close your eyes and listen for a minute." She obeyed, and I closed my eyes as well. From the beach I could hear the roll of the surf, the cries of gulls and sandpipers, the laughter of other vacationers from one of the decks below us. I opened my eyes and looked into Maggie's face, so close to my own. Her eyes were closed—a blue vein, so lovely, so real, throbbed in one of her eyelids in rhythm to her heart. I whispered: "You hear what I hear right now. In all of my other manifestations, these were sounds made by creatures other than myself. They were interesting, and they even had beauty, but I never heard them the way I am hearing them right now. I think only a few humans ever hear them the way I am hearing them at this very moment—so full of life and beauty that the sensation is almost unbearable."

She opened her eyes and looked at me. "I hear these sounds the same way you do and it's because of you. Max, You've added something to my nature. This may be wrong or it may be what we are supposed to experience with each other, but the sound of those gulls on the beach and the breaking surf are given weight because you're here with me. Even the silence that lies between these sounds is possessed by wonder."

We each stared into the other's eyes for a very long time. In that gaze we held a conversation without words, without sparks. How many human beings, particularly lovers, I wondered, understood the power and depth of such communication? I am unsure what Maggie discovered in me, but in her I saw tension, confusion, sadness, and behind all these emotions, love.

Finally she ducked away. “Max, can we pray together?”

I nodded. She took my hands in hers and closed her eyes again. I watched her face for a moment, and then bowed my head.

As we silently offered adoration and thanksgiving, our interior selves, those creatures without bodies, came together as they always do on such occasions, and our praise and love for the One who had created us, who had brought us into being, became an anthem of joy. This hymn, too, we sang soundlessly together as usual, united, pulsating with happiness. In return, love and joy poured over us, again in the usual way, shining through us, a light brighter than any imaginable here on this planet.

Yet that was all. No sparks from beyond ourselves. No communiqués. No instructions from on high. Not even a whisper regarding the flesh, bone, blood, and nerve prison in which we were so hopelessly incarcerated.

When we looked at each other again, I shook my head. The gesture was needless; Maggie already knew; our union in prayer had yielded no answer or guidance.

“We’re sunk, aren’t we,” she said. Her whisper enhanced the enchantment in her voice. “Doomed. Done for.” She tried to sound lighthearted, but a fissure in her voice betrayed that attempt. Her eyes watered with tears.

“I’m not sure about doomed,” I whispered back. “I just don’t know what to do with you or about you.”

“What can we do, Max? What can we do? I keep thinking all this is going to end for us soon. It will end, and Emily and John will marry, and you and I will be separated from each other forever. Maybe it’s wrong, but I don’t want to leave you that way. Please,” she said, and I wasn’t sure whether she was talking with me or with the Other. "Please. I just want something to remember."

We listened to the ocean roaring, the murmur of a television from one of the other rentals, a few shards of talk from the beach. I felt worn and frayed from thinking about her. Now, with her so close, thinking became even more of a burden, more of a tangle. We had not exhausted our options; we'd had no options from the beginning. Why we had received this assignment in this way made even less sense now than when we'd introduced Emily and John at the wine bar. Why, if it was important to have Emily and John meet each other, did it take the two of us to bring about that encounter? Why must we serve as an example when there were a dozen other ways a single manifestation might have introduced them to the joys and hardships of loving each other? Our master is the master of love, and though I was but a speck of a creature, I refused to believe he had dispatched us on a mission leading to torment, remorse, and despair.

Together Maggie and I had climbed to the top of a rugged mountain. This trek had become a torturous, hybrid blend of joy, delight, sorrow, and regret felt by countless human creatures but never by such as ourselves. Were we now to be left on this barren mountain, lusting after the green and fertile valley below without ever tasting the waters of its sweet springs or the fruits of its lush fields?

I shifted a bit on that hard deck, stretching out my legs, and then Maggie was suddenly in my arms, weeping against my chest. I put my arms around her, and after a time she lifted her head, saw the tears in my eyes, and said: "Why? Why were we manifested this way? Why is everything so awful?"

There was no possible reply. I kissed her on the forehead, then on the cheek. She parted her lips when we kissed together, and I moved to touch her shoulder but my hand instead found her breast. She was naked beneath the shift, and when I touched her she pushed against my fingers. Her other hand stroked my thigh. The feel of her breast and her touch on my bare skin made me wild from wanting her.

"Wait," I said, and pulled away. I caught her hand.

"I don't want to wait anymore."

"No. Wait."

The signal for which we had prayed had arrived, one small pulse, like a beam from one of the myriad of stars over the black ocean below us. The light spoke to me, and I spoke its message to Maggie.

"In four days' time you are to meet me at seven o'clock in the evening at the Basilica in the side chapel. The Chapel of the Assumption. Changes will be made."

"You've had contact?"

I nodded, and with dread and sadness, repeated the message.

Chapter Twenty-Two

Report: Private File: Margaret

At 6:56 on Wednesday evening I came into the flesh sitting on a bench behind the Basilica beneath a statue of the Blessed Virgin. Roses were in bloom around me—the sexton was renowned for his gardener's touch—and the air was sweet and heavy with the fragrance of flowers and mown grass. My hands were resting in my lap on the folds of a white dress, silken to the touch, modern yet formal with its ivory buttons, a hemline just below my knees, and lace covering my shoulders. On my feet were white, low-heeled shoes. Clearly Max and I were to make our goodbyes in style.

For two or three minutes I sat on that bench, looking at the blue mountains in the distance beyond the town and remembering the awful ride back to Asheville from the beach. Max and I were in the back of the car, holding hands but never looking at each other, knowing that one glance might plunge us into open grief, trying instead to keep up a pleasant banter with Emily and John or leaning into each other and feigning sleep, all the while touching, touching, touching, still engulfed by the desire of the previous evening even as we silently bid farewell to that desire.

It was dark when we arrived in Asheville. After being dropped with Max in the parking lot of Chestnut Hills—I begged off John's offer to help carry in the luggage to my fictitious apartment, claiming the place was too much of a mess—we waved our goodbyes as Emily and John drove away. As soon as the car turned into the road, I broke down weeping again. So this is a broken heart, I thought: this is how these poor wretches feel when hope is lost, when despair has kicked them in the gut and ripped them apart. They break and weep because no bandage, no medicine, no salve exists for mending such a horrific wound. All hope has vanished, and endurance is the only cure.

Max stepped closer to me. He touched my shoulder, bent close to my face as if to say something or to kiss me, but there it ended. My last picture was his face, shadowy in the dim light, looking at me with love.

Now, in the courtyard of the Basilica, I stood and walked across the grass to the stairs leading up to the church.

Once inside, I paused to allow my eyes to adjust to the dim light. In the Blessed Sacrament chapel at the front of the church two women knelt side by side in prayer. In one of the pews behind them sat a bearded man wearing a bandana, bent forward in prayer or sleep, a large, tattered backpack sticking up above the pew beside him.

To the left of the main altar, standing in the Marian Chapel, was Max. He was facing the small altar, his head bowed, seemingly absorbed in prayer before the statue of the Assumption. As I drew near to him, however, I saw he was staring not at the statue, but at his open palm. Hearing my footfalls, he closed his hand and shoved some object into his pocket.

Like me, Max was dressed somewhat formally for our farewell: blue shirt, off-white linen blazer, peach-colored tie, and khaki trousers. Only when I entered the tiny chapel did he turn fully toward me. I was moving to embrace him when the sight of his faced stopped me in my tracks. Despite our days at the coast, he was as pale as I'd ever seen him. He gave me a sort of sickly smile.

"Max, what's the matter? Are you ill?"

"Something strange—" He broke off, removed his hand from his pocket, and looked at me with a wild confusion in his eyes. "Something muzzy—"

“Muzzy?’ I repeated.

“It’s a blend of muddled and fuzzy.” He seemed a million miles away.

“Muzzy?”

“It’s an antique word, but still appears in standard dictionaries.” He looked at me, then at the statue, then at me again. He patted his pocket. “We…that is, I…there seems to be….”

Clearly something was amiss. Incoherence was foreign to Max. But what came next was even worse. He looked at me again, straight in the eye, and I was beginning another meltdown into tears when he burst into wild laughter. That laughter boomed in the quiet basilica. The acoustics there are such that a penny dropped on the floor near the vestibule rings loud as a bell at the altar, and the poor man with the backpack jerked awake.

“How dare you!” I hissed at Max, keeping my voice low. “Here we are meeting for the last time, and you—”

Max held up one hand, silent now, but still convulsed from laughter. “Wait,” he gasped. “Just let me…sorry…can’t help it….”

I wanted to smack him.

Then all of a sudden he regained control of himself, and his swing from hilarity to abrupt sobriety was so instantaneous that I questioned his sanity. “Are you nuts? What on earth are you thinking? Here we are together for the last time, and all you can do is laugh. Don‘t you know how I—”

And there I stopped. The joy on his face and the love in his eyes slapped me like a cup of cold water. Never had I seen him happier—he glowed with joy, as if that spark inside him, the real Max, was shining like a miniature sun through the pores of his skin. Perhaps he truly had descended into madness. Was insanity part of the script? Feeling concern for him, I touched his arm. “Max, it will be all right. We’ll be all right. Someday a long time from now we won’t remember any of this. Maybe it will all seem like some distant dream. We—”

“I think we’re going to remember everything. Now and forever. Or at least for a long, long time.”

He was, as I say, shining with joy. As manifestations, we give off light sometimes when we appear to humans, but we are never aware of it. Such illumination is our normal state, and so passes unnoticed by us, yet somehow I could now detect this light in Max.

"What's happened to you, Max? What's wrong with you?"

"Nothing's wrong, my dear, sweet Maggie. Nothing at all. I'm not sure everything's right, but nothing's wrong. Not now. It's just very, very strange. I don't understand it and maybe you and I will never understand it, but I don't think it matters much. We'll be different, but somehow all will come to pass and we'll make our way in the world and in the heavens. Earth and heaven—all very strange."

"Max, you're babbling." I felt another impulse to slap him, this time to bring him to his senses.

"Ah, Maggie," he said, and stepped closer and took my hand. His behavior was frightening me, but then his fingers wrapped themselves in mine just as they had all those other times, and my fear disappeared.

But my confusion remained. "Max, you're not making sense. You're—"

He lifted my hand to his lips and kissed my fingers. His smile seemed to fill the shadowy chapel with light.

And then, without taking his eyes from mine, he dropped to one knee. I bent over him, afraid that he was about to faint.

"Margaret," he whispered. "Maggie. We have come on a long journey, you and I. We didn't know the purpose of the journey or how or where or when it would end, and we still don't know. But we do know what has happened between us. We've fought it, we've resisted our natural feelings in a dozen battles, but now that war is over and we've lost. Or perhaps we've won." He smiled. "I'm not sure we'll ever know that either."

"I know, Max," I said, and touched his face. He felt more real at that instant than ever before.

"No," he said. "You don't know." He gently squeezed my hand. "Mary Margaret Hart, will you marry me?"

I stared at him, sickened by his impudence, his jesting at such a time, his mockery. I tried to break free of his hand, but when he wouldn't let go, I began to cry. "Max, this isn't funny. This isn't you. I know you don't—you can't—mean it. Please don't do this—not now, not this last evening together. It's hurting me. Don't make jokes. Please don't make jokes."

"It's no joke. I am asking for your hand in marriage."

Slowly, shaking my head, I knelt on the floor with him and touched his face again and looked at that brilliant smile. "Max, I know you can't help whatever has gone wrong with you tonight. But please, please, please just stop."

"Wait," he said, and after fumbling around he retrieved what he had earlier concealed from me. "I found it in my pocket," Max said. "Since there's no one else here this evening, I do believe it's meant for your finger."

With those words he opened his fingers. On the palm of his hand lay a ring. The diamond reflected the chapel twilight, and glimmered with responsibilities and promises.

That ring, so tiny and delicate in Max's hand, held my eyes like a flame. "That ring was in your pocket?"

"Along with a few more items." He shifted on his knee and said: "I'm asking you again, Mary Margaret Hart. Will you marry me?"

The enormity of his question, of the event, thundered into me and left me weak as water. I leaned my head into his shoulder and began weeping again.

Now he did tease me. "Now, now," he said. "I'm really not that unsuitable a companion, though I don't know whether I'll snore or leave my socks on the bedroom floor. I'm sure you could become accustomed to me over time."

I leaned back, my hands on his shoulders, damp with my tears, and then touched his face, patting his cheek as if to make sure he was real, that we were real.

"Is that a yes?"

"Yes," I said. "Oh, yes, Max. But what does it all mean? How do we know we're supposed to do it?"

"I told you. The ring was in my pocket when I was manifested. May I?"

"May you what?"

"Put the ring on your finger."

"Yes."

It fit perfectly. "It's beautiful, Max." I turned my hand, the ring sparkling in the shadows of the dim-lit chapel.

But Max wasn't looking at the ring. "It pales in comparison to you."

"That's hokey, Max. Especially for you."

"Hokey? And here I thought I was being romantic. Hokey. The word sounds juvenile. Once we're married, we're going to work on your vocabulary."

"Once we're married, we're going to work on loosening you up. When do you think we should get married, by the way?"

"I think, Miss Maggie, we're supposed to kiss before we say much of anything else."

He leaned into me, and I put my hands around his face and kissed him. All the time I was aware of the ring on my finger, the metal band so alien to my flesh and yet such a token of love, an announcement of a future, a sign of marvels and miracles. I wondered if all female humans felt this way and how much time was required before the miraculous became the mundane. But then Max's kiss drove that thought away. His lips were soft, and tasted of salt and tobacco.

"You'll need to give up smoking."

"Ah yes. The great post-modernist sin."

"It's bad for you. And you'll taste better without it."

"I don't really care that much about food."

"I was talking about me tasting you."

"Ah," he said, and kissed me again.

When we stopped, I asked him again about a wedding date. "I don't want to wait too long, Max. Something could change or go wrong."

"Oh, I don't think you'll be waiting long at all."

"What do you mean?"

"Well, unless I have misjudged, I think we're supposed to get married tonight."

"Tonight?" I laughed at him. "Don't be ridiculous. Where'd you get that idea?"

He reached into his pocket again and drew out two rings. They were gold with silver-gold slashes cut at intervals into the band. The one intended for me was slightly thinner than the other. I gasped when I saw them—not at their beauty, though they were well-crafted, but simply at the shock of seeing them.

"They were in your pocket?"

"Along with that diamond."

"But that doesn't mean we should get married tonight."

Again and with a patient smile he reached into a pocket of his coat.

"For goodness sakes," I said. "You're like some strange magician."

He pulled out a slip of paper confirming room reservations at the Indigo, the tall, trim hotel at the end of the street. Emily had told me she'd checked once on room prices in that establishment for her family, and found them very expensive.

"The reservations are for tonight."

"Yes," Max said. "Tonight."

"But who would marry us at this hour, Max?"

"I think He's already here."

"Him?"

"That's the one. Just like at every church wedding."

"But I meant a priest."

"I don't think we can be married by a priest."

"Why on earth not?"

"He'll say something along the lines of 'do you take this man' and 'do you take this woman.' I suspect we don't qualify."

"Oh. Yes…I see."

"I think I know what we're supposed to do. If you'll follow my lead, I'll take us into marriage."

He sounded the words casually enough, but there was a hesitation in his tone, a thickness to his voice. I kissed him again, lightly, a butterfly's brush, and he took my hand and led me from the chapel, down the stairs, and to the steps before the main altar. Here a velvet cord forbade entry to the altar.

Max faced me, holding my hands, but then cocked his head, as if listening to instructions. Smiling, he led me farther across the sanctuary to the entrance to the Blessed Sacrament chapel, where the two women were still kneeling before the One. Max stopped just inside the tiny gate, and then whispered: "Wait just a moment."

He left the chapel, re-entered the sanctuary, and approaching the poor soul seated in the pews, bent over him and whispered in his ear. The raggedy man nodded, stood, and followed Max back to the entrance to the chapel, nodding awkwardly to me and twisting his head round toward the pews to make certain his backpack remained safe. In the meantime, Max tapped both of the women on the shoulder, whispered to them one after another, and took my hand when they stood.

"I'm not sure about this, young man," whispered one of the women, grey-haired, plump, dressed in slacks and a white blouse. "It's very irregular."

"Yes," Max said. "Very."

"It may be illicit."

"Perhaps. But not illegal."

"Are you sure?"

"Check the catechism."

The other woman, Hispanic and also plump, was more formally dressed in a green skirt and yellow blouse. She looked at me with bewilderment.

"It is not a joke?"

"No joke," I said.

The raggedy man coughed into his hand and repeated me. "No joke."

"You'll be our witnesses," Max said. "Something may happen. Something you may remember many years from now."

"I'll already remember this many years from now," the casually dressed woman said. "It's weird."

"I don't suppose you could let me have a couple of bucks," the man said. "I'm trying to get back to Tennessee."

"You're not trying to get back to Tennessee," said Max. "But I'll give you some money."

He handed the man a twenty-dollar bill, which surprised him, but Max didn't witness that surprise. Instead, he swung toward me, took both my hands, and smiled, looking directly into my eyes.

As I had done so many times, I wondered again if all human creatures fully understand the power of their eyes. I have heard that direct eye contact is recommended for job interviews or to close a sale, and some observant humans are aware that the eyes can act like perfume or an aphrodisiac in terms of attraction. On this night, at the particular moment, Max's eyes were more than perfume or aphrodisiac; they were, as some saints and poets have written, windows to his soul, and in gazing into him I saw the reflection of myself and of his love for me.

In addition to the three humans, The One who had made us was there on the altar, both in the Blessed Sacrament and in us. With The One stood a host of those creatures who, like Max and me, had been created spirits without bodies. Though a manifestation, I could still feel the light and warmth of these familiars who surrounded us.

"Let us begin," Max said. He paused, closed his eyes, and then opened them again to look into my face. Slowly and deliberately, he spoke the sacred words: "I, Maximilian, take you, Mary Margaret, to be my wife. I promise to be true to you in good times and in bad, in sickness and in health. I will love you and honor you all the days of my life."

For a second I choked back tears. I trembled, and was happy he was holding my hands. He squeezed my fingers, smiling, and I smiled back at him. Speaking slowly as well, I whispered: "I, Mary Margaret, take you, Maximilian, to be my husband. I promise to be true to you in good times and in bad, in sickness and in health. I will love you and honor you all the days of my life."

Max released my hands, reached into his pocket, and drew out the two rings. The light was dimmer here than in the Marian chapel, but the rings glittered even more brightly. Max took my left hand, removed the diamond, slipped the ring onto my finger, and replaced the diamond. "Mary Margaret, take this ring as a sign of my love and fidelity. In the name of the Father, and of the Son, and of the Holy Spirit."

That gold ring produced an odd sensation, a slight stinging as it passed over my knuckle and rested at the base of my finger. From Max I took the other ring, slipped it onto his finger, then raised that hand to my lips and kissed the ring. "Maximilian, take this ring as a sign of my love and fidelity. In the name of the Father, and of the Son, and of the Holy Spirit."

Max bent toward me and kissed me chastely on the lips. I put my hand behind his neck and kissed him back.

With my eyes closed and caught up by what we had just done, I failed to realize what else was happening in the chapel. Then I heard a cry, and broke away from Max to find the two women on their knees, crossing themselves and pale with terror.

"Jesus!" the ragged man said. "Jesus H. Christ!"

"Yes," Max said, easily, though I could see he was startled as well. "Blessed be His holy name."

The chapel had filled with light, as if we were standing in a noonday sun on a city street. The light emanated from Max, from me, and from The One on the altar.

Both women were praying and had covered their faces with their hands. The homeless man dropped to his knees alongside the women, but had the courage to look at Max. "Who are you, man? What are you?"

Max lay his left hand on the man's head, the ring glowing in all that light, and the man began crying, bending forward until his forehead touched the floor.

The light died as abruptly as it had come alive. The chapel fell back into its evening shadows. One of the women took her hands away from her face and opened her eyes.

"You are my wife," Max said

"And you my husband."

"I think it's a good time to go."

"Whither thou goest, I will go."

He laughed softly, looked again at the kneeling creatures on the chapel floor, and said, "Farewell, all." He genuflected to the altar, I did the same, and we walked toward the back of the church. Behind us the warmth of the celestial host slowly diminished and faded away.

Outside the church, the July twilight, shimmering with heat and noise, filled with the mingled odors of cut grass and exhaust fumes, struck me like a great wave. Everything had changed, had become more vivid, more real. That elderly man across the street licked his lips, and I could see his pink tongue glistening. A long-legged young woman, wearing a tight miniskirt and a white blouse, glanced at us as she passed the courtyard, and the beauty of her tanned face took my breath. The stones of the courtyard pulled me down and made me heavier.

My knees buckled, and though Max kept me from falling, I saw that he too felt the impact of this altered reality. "Max," I said. "What's happened to us?"

Holding my hand, he steadied himself with his other hand on the brick wall, breathing deeply. "We're changing," he said. "We've gone deeper into our manifestations than we've ever gone before—I suppose from getting married just now. I think—I think we've become more real, more truly human. Be patient—I'm sure we'll adjust in another minute or so."

And he was right: slowly our flesh accepted the new depths of our sea-change. Our breathing came easier, our limbs grew steadier. The fluttering sensation—like a sort of motion sickness—passed, and the world about us lost some of its vivid impact.

"What now?" I asked.

Chapter Twenty-Three

Private Report: Maximilian

What now indeed?

"The time is getting on," I said. "I suggest checking in at the hotel."

"Won't the clerk wonder why we have no bags?"

"Hotel clerks see all sorts. Fortunately, their job is to rent rooms rather than act as private investigators. I don't think we have to worry about luggage." Then I pulled the final object from the pocket of my coat: a single electronic key. I pushed one of the three buttons, and a three-year-old Honda Accord in the parking lot just beyond the rectory flashed its lights.

I took Maggie by the hand and swung down the street to the lot. Two blocks away was the Indigo, all glass and pale brick, an anomaly among the older buildings of the neighborhood. When we reached the Accord, I pushed another button and popped the trunk. Inside were two identical black suitcases, a small metal briefcase, and a manila envelope. "The suitcases clearly belong to us," I said, reading our names on the attached labels. Briefly, I examined the contents of the envelope. "Social security cards. My degree in law. Your degree in nursing and an I.D. card showing you as employed at Mission Saint Joe's as a pediatric nurse. Some other trifles."

"And the brief case?"

I released the clasp on the front of the case and opened it. Inside were stacks of bills—twenties and fifties, bound neatly into bundles by rubber bands. With the money was a checkbook showing a deposit at Suntrust Bank.

"What's up with this, Max?"

"It's our start-up money. To get us off the blocks and into the race. It's not as much as it looks. Life is costly here. We'll have to be frugal and work hard."

"I can be very frugal, I think."

"We should consider postponing a honeymoon."

"I don't mind. But I don't want to work as a nurse, Max. I'd like to help you get started instead. You'll need an assistant. I could also help decorate your office."

I smiled at her. Maggie was already sounding very much like a wife.

She smiled back, but seemed troubled. "What now?" she asked again.

"There. The hotel."

"No, Max. I mean what happens to us now."

"I have no idea." I took her hand and squeezed her fingers, offering reassurance, but her expression remained grave.

"Do you feel different, Max? Now that we're married?"

"I feel—I suppose I feel settled."

"Settled?"

"That sounds boring, doesn't it? Yet right now it's the most exciting thing I can imagine. The universe has clicked, some plan of which we are a part is underway, and we now know the path even if we haven't a clue as to what the path holds in store for us. Right now, I'd say all we can do is to follow the path, be brave, and keep our heads up."

"Does the path include a drink?"

"A drink?"

"A glass of champagne is traditional."

"Then let's be off."

We parked at the hotel and entered the lobby carrying our bags. "There's the bar," I said. "And here we are. Now remember, dear—behave yourself."

Maggie punched me lightly on the arm.

Behind the gleaming desk the clerk took my reservation form, poked at his computer, and handed me the form and two plastic keys. "The suite is ready for you, Mr. Lamb. If you need anything—anything at all—please call down."

"Thank you."

We carried our luggage into the bar. The place was gleaming and immaculately clean. Several business types sat at the bar itself, letting down after a day's negotiations, and tourists filled the small tables, sitting with that air of satisfaction and exhaustion derived from a day's exploration. As we found an empty table beside the window facing the street, I noticed that we had become the object of some scrutiny. I wondered at those open glances until I saw our reflection in the window. We still exuded light and love, and might as well have been naked in what we were feeling at that moment toward each other.

Maggie in particular aroused considerable attention. Innocence coupled with the flesh coming alive, naivety joined at the hip with pulchritude, a combination of a blessed virgin with Aphrodite rising from the sea: she carried all these images to the table, where I pulled out her chair and took my place beside her. We held hands across the table. "You've turned quite a few heads."

"I'd say we've both turned a few heads tonight. In addition to losing our own. Oh, Max, I'm so happy." She glanced at her reflection in the window and frowned. "I do want to lose just a little weight, Max."

"Not too much. I like you just the way you are."

"Can we afford a gym membership?

"I'm sure we can." I laughed softly, filled with wonder at what was taking place between us.

The waiter brought the champagne. I filled our glasses and toasted Maggie. "To us," I said. "And to you, my beautiful bride."

We clicked our glasses together and drank.

"Oh, Max. This tastes delicious."

She was right. The drink tasted sharper and more pungent than any I had consumed in my other manifestations. The bubbles tickled my nose, and the aroma went straight to my head. Indeed, all of my senses were sharpened to a degree I had never previously experienced: the humming conversations of the bar's patrons, the glow of bottles behind the bar, the vivid twilight beyond the glass.

Even Maggie was altered in her appearance. She seemed softer somehow, and the more I looked at her, the more my desire for her deepened. Suddenly I had a thought. To give her courage at what I was about to test, I took her hand. She was raising her glass to her lips and smiled at me, then gave me a quizzical look.

"What is it?"

"Send me a spark, please."

"Why would I do that, Max? We're together now."

"Just try it. Send me a spark."

She was silent. Her fingers tightened in my hand. Her lips—those beautiful lips—parted a little. She closed her eyes, and fiercely gripped my fingers, holding my hand for several moments. I felt a slight jolt, but nothing more. Maggie released a breath of air, gasped, and sat, somewhat shaken, back against her chair. "I can't do it, Max," she whispered. "You try it."

"I was trying. The same time you were."

"What's happened?"

"For whatever reason we're losing our powers."

"All of them?"

"I suspect so."

"Oh."

"Exactly."

She closed her eyes and made another effort. Nothing. I had the incongruous wish to kiss those closed eyes and so, bending to her face, did so and kissed her on the forehead as well. She opened her eyes, kissed me lightly on the lips, and said, "What are we then, Max? Who are we?"

"We're who we are. Max and Maggie. Maggie and Max Lamb." She smiled when I said that. "I'm not sure what we are, precisely, but here we are."

"Are we still creatures of light?"

"I think so. Our nature can't change. Only the powers."

"I don't understand."

"Let me give an example. Human beings have the power of sight. But some of them lose that power. Losing it doesn't make them any less human."

"But we're somehow creatures of the flesh too?"

"Yes." I pinched her arm in jest. "More fully human."

"Max?"

"Yes, my dear?"

"I want to go upstairs. To our room."

"I'll take the bags. You bring the champagne and the flutes."

"Flutes?"

"It's what humans call champagne glasses."

"Flutes. How strange and beautiful. Max?"

"Yes, my love?"

"What do you think is going to happen next?"

"When we're alone and together?"

"Yes."

"I have no idea," I said as we approached the elevators. "In some myths humans who sleep with gods or demigods burst into flames or become gods and goddesses themselves."

"Well, we're neither gods nor humans. What happens to us?"

"I'm not sure. But we're about to find out."

Chapter Twenty-Four

Final Report: Gabriel

The consummation of their union produced no flames. It did, however, produce a son.

John Sebastian Lamb was born the following March. One month after this birth, John Flyte and Emily Hoffman, Sebastian's godparents, witnessed his baptism in the Marian chapel of the Basilica of Saint Lawrence. A week earlier, John had entered the Church, and he and Emily were engaged to be married in June.

When the Lambs broke the news of their wedding to their friends, John had laughed with surprise and delight, but Emily burst into tears, followed within seconds by Mary Margaret. While both women cried and hugged each other, John and Maximilian observed with sheepish male silence the two weeping females. Once recovered, and once Mary Margaret had apologized again for the elopement and for not inviting them to the ceremony, Emily was full of questions. She wondered how they had gotten round the pre-marital counseling required by the Church, to which Maximilian replied that the one who had married them had overseen that preparation. And how did he propose? Had he knelt? What was she wearing? Were there witnesses?

At one point Emily turned to Maximilian. "So within minutes after the proposal you were married?"

"Long engagements are tedious."

The newly-weds showed financial prudence by foregoing the traditional honeymoon. They spent one more night in the Indigo, packed the car, and searched for living quarters and an office for Maximilian. That very afternoon they rented a small Victorian home on Chestnut Street, and for two weeks they camped out in the house, visiting thrift shops for everything from cutlery to furniture. A second-hand furniture store delivered a bed, sofa, chairs, bookshelves, and two desks for the downstairs office.

By the middle of August, Hart and Lamb had opened for business. Mary Margaret worked the front desk, answering the phone, greeting clients, and keeping the accounts. After much reading and experimentation, she built a website promoting the practice. Maximilian practiced law, specializing in driving violations and light criminal cases. In the evenings they read together, went dancing or to the movies, or visited with Emily and John. At the Easter Vigil, Maximilian stood sponsor to John when he joined the Catholic Church. Though invited, none of John's relatives attended the ceremony.

With the birth of Sebastian, Mary Margaret and Maximilian experienced that sea change of life brought by parenthood. Mary Margaret continued to assist Maximilian, but as the baby grew, demanding more of her time, she hired an older woman, Anne, to serve both as secretary and baby sitter.

Not everything came easily for them. In the years following Sebastian's birth, Mary Margaret miscarried twice. The second of these miscarriages occurred when the baby, a boy, was nearly full-term, and the couple was heart-broken.

Despite Maximilian's assurances that "I like you just the way you are," Mary Margaret continued to regard herself as overweight, and attempted different diets and exercise plans, all to little avail. Though he occasionally slipped, Maximilian did manage to put to bed his smoking habit. (He was fond of quoting Mark Twain, who famously said, "I have given up smoking—hundreds of times.") The couple suffered all the minor inconveniences of daily modern life; they were sick with the flu for a week when Sebastian was two, Mary Margaret badly dented the car pulling into the narrow garage in the back yard, Maximilian once dropped a gin-and-tonic onto his laptop, and they were forced to cope with the inconveniences that accompany a drafty, creaky, one-hundred-year-old house. They lived, in short, like many other young adults in their circumstances, grounded in the troubles and triumphs of the present day but always with an eye on the future.

When Sebastian was four, Maximilian surprised Mary Margaret by arranging a trip to Italy. "It's the honeymoon you never got."

"Oh, Max, that's so sweet."

"We'll go the week after Christmas," he said. "We'll celebrate all those Church feast days, and I can show you the sights."

"Doesn't Sebastian need a ticket?"

"I've arranged for him to stay with Emily and John."

"I don't know...."

"He'll be fine, Maggie. He loves them and he'll have a brilliant time playing with Henry and Claire."

"I wasn't thinking of him. I was thinking of me."

Maximilian pulled her to his chest and kissed her on the forehead. "You'll be fine too."

On December 26, the feast day of Saint Stephen, they flew into Rome and remained five days in the Eternal City, visiting churches, ruins, and restaurants. They then rented a car and drove north for three days to view paintings in Florence and religious sites in Assisi. As they neared Florence, snow began falling, and they left the main road near the city of Arrezo to enjoy the countryside and to scout out a place for lunch. On this secondary road, the driver of a grocery lorry, a middle-aged man exhausted by worries over a wayward daughter, fell asleep at the wheel of his vehicle, crossed the lane, and smashed headlong at fifty miles per hour into the small Fiat. Maximilian and the driver of the truck expired at the scene of the crash. Six hours later, having never regained consciousness, Mary Margaret succumbed to her injuries in the local hospital. She died unaware that she was carrying a baby girl.

With monies from life insurance and with a will drawn by Maximilian designating Emily and John his caretakers, Sebastian is growing up in a home of love and comfort. He is a hardy little boy, fully human and handsome with his mother's hazel eyes and his father's high cheekbones.

It is recommended that Mary Margaret and Maximilian be given some time for rest and recovery before returning to their duties as guardians and guides.

A few further observations are in order. First, Maximilian incorrectly surmised that he and Mary Margaret were part of an experiment. The One whom many human beings call the Trinity is not a scientist in a laboratory. The One knows all and sees all in all of time, but to all creatures of reason he grants the gift of free will. Mary Margaret and Maximilian were dispatched only to assist the two subjects: John Flyte, who was in despair and in danger of losing his capacity for loving God, and Emily Hoffman, who had nearly abandoned all hope for true love. Maximilian and Mary Margaret were manifested to aid them, to allow them a chance for faith and true affection. That these two manifestations then fell in love with each other was pure happenstance. Their mutual attraction surprised their controllers as much as it did them. What The One made of the situation I do not know.

We expected to recall them, but directions to do so never arrived. Such a recall, I suspect, would have violated a basic principle of Creation. As another human being, also named John, had written twenty centuries earlier, God is love. The love that took root and flourished between Mary Margaret and Maximilian, though unique in our annals, was nonetheless love. And as that love grew between them, it became what another human being by the name of Paul described so long ago: their love was patient and kind; it did not envy, it did not boast, it was not proud. Their love was not rude, it was not self-seeking, it was not easily angered, it kept no record of wrongs. Their love rejoiced with the truth. It always protected, always trusted, always hoped, always persevered. Their love never failed.

This is the love beloved by the Creator.

It was this love that prompted our gifts of assistance: the camping supplies for Graveyard Fields, the rings in Maximilian's coat pockets at the Basilica, the tools in the trunk of the car required for entry into the world.

Though they lost their special celestial powers, Mary Margaret and Maximilian lived those next years as manifestations. More than the rest of us who engage in this work, they came to understand the agonies and joys of human love. They realized how desire feeds desire, how love with its attendant pains and pleasures is more tangled, more complex, and more beautiful than any of the mathematical formulae by which the universe operates. For millennia, all of us—seraphs, cherubim, and guardians in heaven, and on earth poets, philosophers, scientists, and ordinary men and women—have tried to understand and come to grips with this force we call love, and yet love remains as profound a mystery as the One who brought love into being in the first place.

Everyone who has ever loved has known what love is. Yet not one of us can explain it.

Chapter Twenty-Five

Spark: Max?

Spark: Hello, my dear Maggie.

Spark: How are you?

Spark: Just back from the Levant, where I was giving strength and consolation to a physician ordered beheaded for his religious beliefs.

Spark: Oh.

Spark: He died praying. He died bravely. And you?

Spark: I was in Poughkeepsie. An eight-year-old boy grieving the death of his mother from a brain aneurysm.

Spark: And you consoled him?

Spark: I tried, Max. We shall see. He made me think of Sebastian. I decided that since I was in the neighborhood, I would stop by and see our son.

Spark: Poughkeepsie and Asheville are hardly in the same neighborhood.

Spark: Oh, Max. Don't go all stuffy on me.

Spark: So how is Sebastian?

Spark: He's grown again since you saw him at Christmas, Max. Emily and John are raising him well. He'll be eight in March. In May he makes his first communion. I thought we might be there.

Spark: If it is permitted.

Spark: If it is permitted. Oh, Max, I miss him.

Spark: Sometimes I can still feel his arms around my shoulders and his breath on my cheek.

Spark: Remember the Sky Bar and the storm? Remember the beach? Do you remember, Max?

Spark: I remember all of it. I remember how the sunshine felt when I kissed you by the fountain. I remember the hip bumps and the touch of your fingers in mine.

Spark: So do I. And I feel all of it too. I thought we weren't supposed to remember the feelings. Just the actions.

Spark: We aren't supposed to remember the feelings.

Spark: But we remember, you and I.

Spark: All the time.

Spark: And you miss everything the way I do?

Spark: All the time.

Spark: I miss it all so much. I miss our morning coffee together and watching you read books and hearing your voice and watching Sebastian learn to walk. I miss the way he looked when he was sleeping and the way he smiled and the way he made you laugh when the two of you played hide-and-seek. But mostly I miss touching the two of you and holding you. Do you miss those things, Max?

Spark: All the time.

Spark: It's the oddest sensation. Missing him and you and everything else we had together makes me sad and happy at the same time.

Spark: Yes.

Spark: You're unusually quiet.

Spark: I am remembering everything.

Spark: Max?

Spark: I'm here.

Spark: I love you.

Spark: I love you too, Maggie.

Acknowledgements

Dust On Their Wings, an entertainment about romance, passion, and love, has many authors. My students, my friends, my family, especially my children and grandchildren: all have encouraged me in my writing, mostly in ways unknown to them. I am grateful for the joy and inspiration they have given me.

Three young women—Miller Voigt, Katie Kania, and Bonnie Gibson, all former students—deserve my special thanks for their help in bringing this book together. Each of them had a hand in the editing and production of *Dust*. They strengthened the book. Whatever mistakes remain belong to me alone.

Made in the USA
Las Vegas, NV
20 February 2024

86034302R00138